"A NOVEL OF IDEAS, NO LESS, THOUGH IT REACHES THE BRAIN VIA CHILLS UP THE SPINE."
L.A. WEEKLY

"There is much to be enjoyed. . . . Mystery, Gothic horror, social satire, black comedy and stories of the double are skillfully woven together."
The New York Times Book Review

"Patrick McGrath [has a] talent for introducing the truly weird with a quiet and creepy nonchalance. . . . Much of the pleasure of THE GROTESQUE arises in savoring its layer upon layer of uncertainty, even while McGrath's plot— a country house murder and its consequences— seems perfectly straightforward. The background is lovingly elaborated. . . . THE GROTESQUE really thrills as a study in narrative technique."
The Washington Post Book World

"Extraordinary . . . A cross between *Turn of the Screw* and one of Iris Murdoch's great gothic tales . . . A wonderfully inventive, sinister, macabre yet comic portrait of England in decay . . . McGrath is a masterful prose stylist, THE GROTESQUE is high art."

John Hawkes

"Bizarre, comical, and quite suitably tilted . . . [A] wonderfully eccentric narrative—controlled by McGrath's precise, measured prose . . . Entertaining, absorbing, grotesquely comic and comically grotesque."
The Cleveland Plain Dealer

THE GROTESQUE

A Novel

Patrick McGrath

BALLANTINE BOOKS • NEW YORK

Library of Congress Catalog Card Number: 89-3486

ISBN 0-345-36407-4

This edition published by arrangement with Poseidon Press, a
division of Simon & Schuster, Inc.

Manufactured in the United States of America

First Ballantine Books Edition: December 1990

ORSOLYÁNAK
(FOR ORSOLYA)

Nature is a temple in which living columns sometimes emit confused words. Man approaches it through forests of symbols, which observe him with familiar glances.
—Baudelaire

I HAVE HAD much leisure in the past months to reflect on my first encounter with Fledge, and why he formed such an immediate and intense antipathy toward me. Butlers, I think, are born, not made; the qualities of a good butler—deference, capability, a sort of dignified servility—are qualities of character that arise in cultures where a stable social hierarchy has existed, essentially undisturbed, for centuries. One rarely encounters a good butler in France, for instance, and a good American butler is a contradiction in terms. Fledge is not a born butler; he does not, by nature, defer, nor does he naturally serve. There is in him, at a quite deep level, I believe, a furious resentment that he should be doing this work. Not that one can detect it in the man's behavior, but it's there all the same. It has become apparent to me not only that he felt humil-

1

iated by what he was doing, but that he bore toward me a fierce antagonism for being the instrument of it. I was not particularly sympathetic; if he enters my house as a butler, I thought, then I shall treat him as a butler. How could I have guessed the lengths to which his ambition would drive him?

All this I have reconstructed since being confined to a wheelchair. At the time I was aware only of a certain emanation from the man, and I remember thinking that though he was a bit bloody-minded, a bit *bolshie*, if he made Harriet happy then I could quite easily put up with a spot of subdued rancor, as long, of course, as it stayed subdued. After all, I thought, what truck did I have with the man? To a large extent I lived in the barn with my bones, and when in the house I needed him only to put plates of food and glasses of drink under my nose. Let him be bolshie, I thought (by no means selflessly), if he keeps Harriet happy. As a connoisseur of ironies, I cannot, now, help recognizing just how rich this one is.

Since the onset of paralysis I have lost weight, and my tweeds these days hang limp and baggy from my stick-thin frame. My face, too, has changed, as I have ascertained from those fleeting glimpses I catch of it while being wheeled past a mirror. I am humped and cadaverous; my hands lie clawlike on the arms of the wheelchair, and my eyes gaze blankly from a bony, sunken head whose jaw has come permanently to rest upon my clavicle. But in the days of which I speak I held my head upright, and from my steel-gray eyes there leaped sparks of fierce intelligence, no less fierce, in fact, than the barbs of wit that rose constantly to my rather thin and mocking lips. I had a sharp and aquiline nose (I still do), a *patrician* nose, I always thought it, and atop a clear and lofty brow my thick black hair sprang sideways with oily, crinkly, irrepressibly shaggy energy.

This, then, is what I looked like as I strode briskly into the drawing room that fateful morning last autumn, to find Sidney Giblet leaning against the mantelpiece with a glass of my sherry in his hand, while Harriet and Cleo, also drinking sherry, were sprawled in armchairs, and popular music of some sort came out of the gramophone. "Here you are, darling," said Harriet. "What about some sherry? Sidney has been telling us about the death of Rupert Brooke."

I snorted inwardly. The death of Rupert Brooke—this was quintessential Sidney. On the far side of the room, over by the drinks cabinet, I noticed the new butler. I remember feeling, even then, a twinge of unease. Dome, you see, had been so old and helpless, much of the time we had had to wait on *him*! "I believe he was assaulted by a mosquito," I said dryly, "and died of his wounds."

"Oh Daddy," cried Cleo, "don't be so horrid."

"It's true," said Sidney, who was clearly in truckling mood, and eager to avoid conflict. "He saw no action, and died in bed of an infection."

"An infection," said Cleo, sadly. "And him so keen on cleanness."

I grinned wolfishly at this rich irony, and Sidney glanced at me uneasily. I think what irritated me most about Sidney, apart from his shrill laughter and his vegetarianism, was his pipe. He smoked a little pipe with

3

a slender reddish rosewood stem and a petite bowl that
took no more than a pinch or two of delicately scented
herb tobacco—I am not making this up, he smoked herb
tobacco! It may, in fact, it now occurs to me, have been
his very daintiness, his weediness, that attracted Cleo
to him; have you noticed how often vivacious women
are attracted to spineless types of men? It's a phenomenon one frequently observes in Nature, particularly
among the insects. For weeks now Sidney had been
fluttering about the dark-paneled rooms of Crook like
some rare and exotic butterfly, trailing his delicate pipe
fumes behind him and generally being a pest. I should
have liked to throw him out, but of course I couldn't,
for Cleo apparently had feelings for the creature. "Tell
us more," I said, as the new butler appeared at my
elbow with a silver tray upon which stood an infinites-
imal glass of sherry, "about Rupert's infection. You,"
I said, turning to the butler, "must be Fledge."

"I'm *so* sorry, darling," cried Harriet, rising to her
feet, "how silly I am! Of course he is; and Fledge, this
is Sir Hugo."

He bowed.

"Now Fledge," I said, "you will have to learn about
sherry. One does not drink it from a thimble. Bring me
a *glass* of sherry, please."

He made another bow and returned to the drinks cabinet. Harriet, who clearly intended that the man's ini-
tiation to life at Crook should be a happy one, joined
him there, and began whispering, doubtless instructing
him in the alcoholic idiosyncrasies of the master.

"Oh, I know very little about it," said Sidney, with
a sigh. "I believe the doctors were to blame—they mis-

diagnosed him, or some such thing. I believe it was very painful at the end.''

I beamed at Cleo, who shivered quite dramatically, her girlish imagination having already transported her to the hero's deathbed, out there in the barbarous Aegean. Then Fledge reappeared with a proper glass of sherry, and before insisting that the gramophone be turned off I proposed a toast to mosquitoes everywhere.

Sidney seemed unwilling, at lunch, to talk more about the nature of Rupert Brooke's infection, probably out of consideration to Cleo. I don't go for this, myself; I always think it's a mistake to pander to the squeamishness of women. Disease, infection, rot, filth, feces, maggots—they're all part of life's rich weft and woof, and anyone with a properly scientific outlook should welcome such phenomena as facets of Nature every bit as wonderful as golden eagles and oak trees and great rift valleys and the like. I think the family of a scientist, particularly, should not be permitted to discriminate among Nature's variety, and to press home this point it was in those days my habit over coffee to send for Herbert.

Herbert was a toad, and I kept him in a glass tank in my study. Because I fed him well, and he did not take much exercise, he was extremely large. I did not find him monstrous, however, nor was there anything revolting to me in the spectacle of a toad eating maggots at the dinner table. These maggots (which are produced by the eggs of the cheese-fly, *Piophila casei*) George Lecky, my gardener, collected for me on the pig farm down in Ceck's Bottom. I would spill a few of them onto my plate and watch Herbert set to. Harriet and

Cleo had long ago learned to ignore this ritual, and Sidney, whom I generally took the opportunity of instructing in the reproductive and other habits of the species, never knew quite where to look, or how much enthusiasm he had to affect to keep me happy. I do admit that Harriet's distaste for the toad was not altogether groundless. Her father, the colonel, you see, was called Herbert, and I had somewhat mischievously suggested to her on an earlier occasion that my little beast bore a passing resemblance to the old man, who was, in point of fact, remarkable for his warts. Somehow, and to Harriet's chagrin, the name had stuck.

So it was, then, that after Fledge had poured and served the coffee I told him to bring Herbert to the table.

"Sir?" he said. Harriet, clearly, had not mentioned Herbert when she outlined the man's duties to him.

"Oh *no*, Hugo, *please*," she said.

"My dear," I said, "didn't you tell Fledge about Herbert? Come, Fledge," I said, rising to my feet and dabbing at my lips with a starched white napkin, "and meet Herbert."

Fledge was soon instructed in the proper method of extracting Herbert from his tank, and bringing him to the dining room; and though I could tell the man had no natural feeling for toads, he showed not a flicker of distaste at performing the, to him, disgusting task. Soon Herbert was established on the table, with a big plateful of squirmy white maggots in front of him. I told Sidney that it was once thought that toads were poisonous, but the secretion in question was in fact merely a sort of defensive slime that is highly unpleasant to predators.

"Really?" said Sidney, and set down his coffee untasted. It was at that point that I noticed the butler's eyes upon me, glinting, for the first time, from beneath hooded lids, with unmistakable hostility; but no sooner had I apprehended the fact than he shifted his glance and continued about his duties.

After lunch I returned to the barn and had, I seem to remember, rather a good afternoon with the leg.

THE BRAIN IS poorly comprehended by our doctors, though none of course care to admit just how profound is their ignorance. They prefer to gloss over the gulfs in their knowledge with jargon—screeds of verbiage that never explain, only occasionally describe, and generally obfuscate. Take this, for instance: "Damage to the posterior sectors of the inferior frontal convolution of the patient's left hemisphere may have been the cause of the disintegration of his capacity for speech." It was my damaged convolution they were referring to here, but could any of them explain to me (even if they thought it worth the effort, which they didn't) why certain mental faculties were spared, and the rest frozen? Why am I able to see, know, and evaluate the world, yet lift not a finger, nor even *blink* at will? They don't know. In fact, they don't even know that I am capable of experience. Only Cleo does; and possibly Fledge.

Consciousness can be inferred only from behavior, and as I produced no behavior after my "cerebral accident" (about which more in due course), I remained to all intents and purposes a vegetable. No one ever actually called me a vegetable, not within my hearing; but there are other ways of saying it. Toward the end of my hospitalization I remember being wheeled out in front of a group of medical students in order that certain points about catalepsy could be made. It was remarked by a neurologist called Dendrite, who took an occasional interest in me, that I lacked "mental presence," that I was "ontologically dead." He went on to describe what he called the "clinical picture." He referred to my "severe masking," to my "cataleptic fixity of posture," to my compulsive grimace, my grinding teeth, my stertorous breathing, accompanied, he said, by "guttural phonation not unlike the grunting of a pig." Mortified as I was by this last remark, it did not cut me as had the reference to my ontological deadness. What torture, after all, could compare to an experience of isolation like mine? I, ontologically dead? I was, I believe, the most ontologically *alive* person in that room.

This, then, is the "I" who speaks: cocooned in bone, I pupate behind a blank and lizardlike stare, as my body is slowly consumed by its own metabolism. "He is a pitiful, motionless, misshapen man, unwholesome in appearance and destined to vegetate for the rest of his days." My neurologist never actually said this, but he might as well have. As for destiny, I have come to believe that to be a grotesque is my destiny. For a man who turns into a vegetable—isn't that a grotesque?

I seem to remember I was out in the barn the morning the Fledges arrived. I still had the use of my body in those days, I was an active man doing hard intellectual work, not so young that I took for granted my own health and vitality, nor old enough to have become preoccupied with them. I was middle-aged, a middle-aged scientist, in fact a paleontologist, an expert on the great carnosaurs of the late Mesozoic era. I was extremely busy at the time, for I had an important lecture to deliver to the Royal Society; this partly explains why I had no part in the hiring of the Fledges. Harriet saw to all that.

Harriet is my wife. I will not pretend that ours has been a happy marriage, and now that I am paralyzed I find myself saddened at what we wasted. The fault is largely mine. Harriet believes the doctors when they tell her I am a vegetable, she has no reason to think otherwise. We created no strong spiritual bond, nothing that might enable us to transcend my paralysis and maintain contact. With Cleo this is possible, but not with Harriet. She makes sure that I am properly attended to by Mrs. Fledge, but except in one important regard her life has not changed dramatically with my condition; you see, from Harriet's point of view I have always in a sense been paralyzed. What *has* changed is that for the first time since our marriage she has become interested in another man. The new man in her life is Fledge.

It was Harriet, as I say, who hired the Fledges. She

went up to London and interviewed them, and came back very impressed. She engaged them on the spot, and I was not very happy about that, as there seemed to be some difficulty with their papers. They'd been in the employ of a coffee planter in Kenya, a man who apparently was trampled by an ox and expired without writing them references. But Harriet was sure there wouldn't be a problem. She had a "feeling" about them, she said. And since the servants' wages come out of her money, not mine, I merely registered an objection and left it at that.

On reflection this strikes me as fairly typical of my involvement in the running of the house—I occasionally registered an objection and left it at that. You see, I had for so long been preoccupied with my bones that I was oblivious to the domestic arrangements that formed the grounds, so to speak, of my existence. I ate, I drank, and I slept in the house, but my passion, my vitality— that was exercised only in the barn. I lived in the barn, I merely existed in the house. This is not to say that I bear no responsibility for what followed. On the contrary, I was derelict, I see that now, in letting Harriet have a completely free hand to staff the house as she saw fit. Though I must say in my own defense that I had never had reason to doubt her judgment; there was never a problem with the Domes.

I was in the barn, then, when the Fledges arrived. I can imagine only too well what happened: Harriet came to the front door and exclaimed: "Mr. and Mrs. Fledge!"—then opened her arms in a brief ceremonial gesture of welcome. She has a way of doing this, a way of greeting visitors, that implies that with their arrival all, at last, is well. It's an endearing trait, and but one manifestation of Harriet's "warmth." Harriet herself, I should perhaps tell you, is small, plump, and fifty, dresses in trim and comfortable tweeds, and her crowning glory is a magnificent head of coppery tresses which she coils in a bun at the back of her skull and fastens with a sort of knitting needle. Her complexion is pink and unblemished, and she has little, nibbling teeth, like a hamster's. Cleo does not take after Harriet at all; Cleo is a true Coal, she takes after me.

Do you detect bitterness here? Am I displaying the suppressed rage that simmers constantly in this dying heart of mine? I cannot deny it; if Harriet had kept her wits about her, if her intuitive faculties had not been dulled long ago by a compulsion to observe what she calls "the proprieties," she would never have brought the diabolical man under my roof, and I would not be in this wheelchair today. But this is wishful thinking. It is not my intention to whine, merely to describe what I have suffered at the hands of a treacherous servant and a faithless wife. You may, when you have heard me out, bestow upon me your sympathy, and then again you may not. It hardly matters; when my story is over I shall be dead.

So. I have told you what Harriet did on the doorstep that morning last autumn; but what sort of a spectacle did the Fledges present, standing there in their long dark overcoats, among their black suitcases? I will tell you: they were like a pair of gaunt and leafless trees.

Fledge himself is difficult to describe. Indeterminacy clings to the man like a mist. He has for so long concealed his true feelings that whatever core of real self yet glows within him, it is invisible to the naked eye. He is neat, of course, in fact he is impeccable, as befits a butler. Slim, slightly over medium height, with reddish-brown hair oiled back at a sleek angle from a peak dead in the middle of his forehead, he could be anything; but the presence at his side of Mrs. Fledge—Doris—situates and defines the man. For Doris is unmistakably a servant. As tall as her husband (and thus a clear head taller than me), thin as a rake, with a sharp, pinched face and black hair scraped back off her forehead and threaded with iron-gray wires, her being is indelibly stamped with the mark of domestic toil. Her nose is prominent and beaky, and her eyes are very dark, iris and pupil both so black they seem fused in a single orb with the merest pinprick of light dead in the center. Those black eyes lend to her face a rather opaque, birdlike quality, and though the simplicity of the woman's nature very soon becomes apparent, at first sight she gives the appearance of a large crow, an unblinking alien to human affairs, a corvine transmigrated into woman's form. Only the tip of her nose, enlivened by a network of tiny broken blood vessels, lends color and humanity to her face. And thus they presented themselves, the ghoul and the crow, and then they were over the threshold and under my roof.

It occurs to me that you may be wondering why we need a butler at all, so I should perhaps explain that this was, for Harriet, an indispensable part of "observing the proprieties." She was brought up in the belief that a house was not a house without some sort of man-servant in it. Not that she's a snob, but she so totally assimilated the outlook of her father, the colonel, that she finds it impossible, in some respects, to adapt to changing social and economic conditions. Failure to adapt, I would tell her, leads to extinction; but she never cared. "Let us die out then," she blithely replied, "but let us at least do it comfortably." Hence the butler. We've always had one, but the last, an ancient fossil called Dome, died of old age in the summer, and his wife followed him to the grave within a fortnight.

Harriet would then have led them down the hall and through to the back of the house, and so to their quarters, a large, low-ceilinged room at the end of a dark, flagstoned passage, adjacent to an ancient bathroom with tarnished brass taps and a hundred-year-old lavatory. Having been installed in these obscure regions, the Fledges then, presumably, were shown over the house and had their duties explained to them. By the time the gong went for lunch they had taken root.

What else should you know before we go on? The house is called Crook. It is a sixteenth-century manor house, the basic plan of which is the E-shape, two gabled wings projecting at either end and a porch in the middle. Constructed of brick and timber, the walls are now completely overgrown with ivy, and the windows peer through the foliage like the eyes of some stunted and shaggy beast. There is moss between the roof tiles, and in front of the house the driveway curves round a small pond overgrown with rushes and coated with a thick green scum. To the right of the house a cobblestoned alley leads to the back yard, which is enclosed on two sides by empty stables and outhouses, and on the third, facing the back door, by a brick wall that gives onto the vegetable garden and the orchard. Off to the left of the house stands the barn. Crook, curiously, faces south, a remarkable decision on the part of the builder, given the sixteenth-century belief that the south wind brought corruption and evil vapors. It requires extensive work, particularly the roof, which leaks, and the plumbing, which is not only unreliable but noisy. A flushed toilet rumbles like thunder, in Crook.

House and barn stand in the few acres that remain of a once-sizeable estate; only the pig farm down in Ceck's Bottom has not been sold off, largely because it's not worth anything. Behind the house, to the north, the land drops gently to the valley of the Fling, a narrow, serpentine river that soon slips out of sight on its way to the Ceck Marsh. This is an extensive stretch of wild country that lies beyond the village of Ceck, the spire of whose Norman church is visible over the distant treetops. I shall have more to say about the Ceck Marsh shortly. On the far side of the valley the land begins to climb quite steeply, and here open fields give way to dense woodland, beeches and oaks mainly. The village lies to the east, while to the west the trees gradually thin out to a jumble of copses and dells, among which a famous colony of rocks has long been established. This is abrupt, uneven country, full of hills and woods, and therefore full of birds. Ten miles further west you come to a market town called Pock-on-the-Fling; this is the nearest settlement of any size. Crook itself lies within the parish of Ceck, in the northeast corner of Berkshire, and my story begins in the autumn of 1949.

IT WAS SHORTLY after the arrival of the Fledges that a rather bizarre incident occurred, one to which I paid no more than a cursory attention at the time but which now strikes me as being charged with a sort of eerie, portentous significance. Have I told you that I was to deliver an important lecture to the Royal Society of Paleontology, a lecture concerning a species of late Mesozoic predatory carnivore that I discovered myself in East Africa as a young man, and to whose bone structure I had devoted my entire career? *Phlegmosaurus carbonensis* (so named because the bones came up slightly charred—Greek *phlegein*, to burn) has, I still believe, quite revolutionary implications not only for the science of paleontology but for zoology in general—but I need not weary you with that now. The point is, it was my habit, when I still had the use of my limbs, to think out my lectures in the Ceck Marsh; the silence and the solitude were somehow conducive to mental rigor and clarity, I found.

So one afternoon I set off with a flask of whisky and a stout stick, and after tramping down a soggy cart track between thick growths of birch and alder I found myself beneath a vast gray sky with miles of flat, boggy fen before me and a lake in the distance. The air had a smoky, autumnal tang to it, I remember, and as I picked my way over the rough damp clumps of peat and moss, all tufted with marsh grass and bristling in the wind, and puddled between with rank, black water, my heart exulted at the stillness and desolation of it all. Wildfowl rose from their nests in the weeds and with a great honking flurry went flapping off towards the water, and I came squelching on through in my Wellington boots, with my thick tweed cap pulled low against the bite of the wind.

It was when I had settled myself on a hummock of dry bracken close to the edge of the lake, and was casting my eye idly over the gray, wind-furrowed water, that I noticed a bulky horned object half-submerged in a bed of reeds close by. I splashed forward through the shallows to investigate, and discovered to my astonishment that it was a dead cow. I poked at it with my walking stick, then with the crook of the stick I hooked its horn and dragged it further into the shallows, and as I did so I caused the head to rise and water poured from its empty eye sockets as though from a fountain. Then the great body began to turn, began to go belly-up, and suddenly a foul, nauseating stench was released into the air and a pike, a big one, four feet long, slid out of the cow's belly and gazed at me for an instant, its gills quietly lapping, before gliding away into the depths of the lake.

Not so extraordinary, you will say; but have you ever seen a pike? They have narrow, pointed snouts, and a projecting lower jaw crammed with sharp teeth, and they seem to *grin* at you; and this one was very big, and very old. The construction of their heads is an instance of natural functional design, no more than that, but it tends to make one think them malevolent; and when this one appeared with such sinister suddenness from inside the bloated and foul-smelling corpse of the cow, the gaze of its cold killer's eyes (and pike will eat anything, even their own kind) seemed so charged with malice and evil that my hair, for a moment, quite literally froze on my head. I did not, as I say, take the incident very seriously at the time, beyond, that is, describing it in detail at dinner that night; but often in recent days the picture of that wicked old pike sliding out of the cow's belly has come into my mind, without any apparent pretext.

Just to finish the story, it occurred to me that the dead cow would make good feed for George's pigs, so I tramped off across the marsh in a northeasterly direction, to Ceck's Bottom, and told him about it. And as far as I know it was George's pigs that got the rest of that cow, not the old pike.

I soon made the acquaintance of Doris Fledge, she of the crowlike features and red-tipped nose. In those early days of autumn she cooked us solid, unpretentious meals that always came hot to the table, and I was well satisfied. Maybe Harriet had been right about the Fledges, I thought. Like Darwin I do not care what I eat as long as it's the same every day, and I had been used to depend on old Mrs. Dome (when her rheumatism wasn't "playing up") to put square, English meals before me, meat and vegetables unadulterated by sauces, spices, or savories. Mrs. Fledge was apparently in the same culinary tradition, and this permitted me to devote my mealtimes to reading the *Times*, or thinking about my lecture, or tormenting Sidney Giblet, with no anxieties about what would appear on my plate.

One morning, feeling particularly jaunty before going out to the barn, I decided on impulse to visit the kitchen, and inquire of Mrs. Fledge what was for lunch, and say a kind word or two—a kind word from the master never goes amiss, with servants. I had been out in the vegetable garden with George, who was building a bonfire of dead leaves and other garden rubbish, and as I remember it was a fine, crisp day, which was why I was feeling jaunty. Crossing the yard toward the back door, I glimpsed Mrs. Fledge in the kitchen; she had her back to the window, and was occupied with something at the large oak dresser that fills one entire wall of the room. Even from halfway across the yard there was an unmistakably *furtive* character to the woman's movements, and I remembered a hunch I'd formed about her the first time I clapped eyes on her. Well, I advanced briskly across the yard, my leather-soled brogues ringing out sharp and clear on the dry stones, and she must have heard me, for she quickly moved away from the dresser, and over to the sink, where I

19

found her washing up the breakfast dishes when I came in through the back door.

"Morning Mrs. Fledge," I said.

"Good morning, Sir Hugo," said she, rapidly wiping her hands on the apron lashed tightly about her narrow waist, and looking flustered in a way I rather enjoyed. A strand of silver-threaded hair had escaped her bun, and she pushed it aside with a quick, nervous movement.

"Go on with your work, Mrs. Fledge," I said, airily, striding about the kitchen. "I merely wanted to know what sweetmeats and dainties you planned to tempt us with at luncheon today."

I had fetched up hard by the oak dresser; the woman's fluster increased perceptibly. "Chops, Sir Hugo," she said.

"Splendid! I love a chop. Grilled?"

"Yes, Sir Hugo."

In the middle of the kitchen, which is rather a low room with black beams running across the ceiling, and a flagstoned floor, and a huge black wood-burning stove at the far end, there stands a table of scrubbed oak, and upon it lay a thick bunch of carrots, the soil still clinging to them and their leafy tops splayed greenly across the pale wood, and beside them a bowl of large potatoes, a bowl of onions, and a cabbage. All products of the Crook garden, reared with loving care by that good man George Lecky. "And carrots, Mrs. Fledge?" I said.

"Yes, Sir Hugo." She was standing with her back to the sink, polishing a teacup and positively reeking of guilt. I dug my hands deep in my trouser pockets and approached the woman. As I suspected, it was not only guilt she reeked of—she'd been at my sherry! She must have a bottle stashed in the dresser! I drew close. Terror blazed up in her blackbird eyes. She almost dropped the teacup. From about eighteen inches I gazed into her horror-struck face and examined the delicate lacework of ruptured capillaries on the point of her beak, and smiled. "And onions, Mrs. Fledge?" I said.

"Yes, Sir Hugo." She had frozen rigid. I pushed aside the strand of silver hair that had again worked loose from the bun. I ran my fingers across her cheek, and squeezed her little earlobe. "Jolly good," I said, and sauntered out of the kitchen. I would say nothing yet, I decided. I would choose my moment. There would, I felt sure, come a perfect opportunity to bring up with Harriet the housekeeper about whom she had insisted there would not be a "problem." Your housekeeper, I would say, does have a "problem," Harriet. She "drinks."

I paid particularly close attention to the chops that day, curious as to whether Mrs. Fledge's tippling hampered her performance in the kitchen. They were delicious. They were grilled to perfection. The carrots were thoroughly boiled, and the potatoes flawlessly mashed. Perhaps, I thought, like Churchill she functions best on a steady tipple. I was right, I reflected, to say nothing. I turned to Sidney and asked him what he knew about the life cycle of the bot-fly. The poor dummy blushed scarlet; he had never even heard of the bot-fly, so I told him all about it. Do you know about the life cycle of the bot-fly? *Gastrophilus equi?* It lays its eggs on the forequarters of a horse. When the eggs hatch out, the irritation makes the horse lick the hairs and swallow the larvae. The larvae feed on the inner lining of the horse's stomach for a year, and then lodge in its dung and are excreted. They bury themselves in the ground and pupate—and the process starts all over again. Elegant, no? Elegant, invariable—and pointless.

OF ALL THE various perspectives I am offered by the chance emplacement of my wheelchair, there are two that I particularly favor. The first, a strong contender on warm days, is between the French windows at the far end of the drawing room. From there I can look out over the flower garden, with its terraces and its goldfish pond, its hedges and lawns, all threaded with narrow, winding paths and enclosed by a crumbling brick wall. I used to enjoy watching George work among the flowers there, down on his knees in the soil; he's gone now, of course, and the garden is growing wild without him. No one else gives a damn.

My other favorite is the fireplace. Like a small boy I can gaze for hours into a fire and see cathedrals and monsters, basilisks, dragons, and gorgons; and when I tire of the flames, the elaborate carving of the chimneypiece, which I will describe to you in due course, is an unfailing source of pleasure, and even moral support, in these dark times.

Often, though, my wheelchair is placed with no thought as to the view I will be afforded. I am put before windows that look out onto empty yards, or wheeled into dark corners so that floors can be waxed and carpets swept. Sometimes I end up in the alcove under the stairs, and there is deep irony in this, as you will learn. It occurs to no one but Cleo that I might mind this; they think me a vegetable. So what am I to make of the fact that Fledge quite deliberately turns my wheelchair to the wall? Am I to presume that he does not care for the blank eyes of a vegetable upon him as he goes about his work? Or is it something else? Does he know I'm still thinking, and does he do it, therefore, to intensify my pain? Is it a form of torture? I am inclined to believe that it is.

You see, I believe that even before he entered the front door of Crook—even before he *met* me!—Fledge had conceived the ambition to usurp me. I would hazard that there had always been a seed of discontent, a seed of revolt, in his nature, but that only now, comparatively late (for Fledge is not a young man), had he fully resolved to act on it. "Better to reign in hell," he might have said, like Milton's Satan, "than to serve in heav'n," and it's not hard to see him as a Satan, as a serpent that came slithering into Crook with nothing but evil intentions, though of course it is only by means of the small gestures and fleeting expressions he made that I realize now how intensely, even in those days, he hated me. He *had to* hate me, you see—I doubt he could have gone through with it otherwise. And this is why, today, he turns my wheelchair to the wall: hating me has become a habit.

It's a curious thing how glibly complacent we tend to be about the superiority of the mammal. I remarked earlier, apropos of something or other, that the life cycle of the bot-fly was pointless. I didn't mean it, of course. It would be absurd to suggest that any species has more "point" to it than any other. The natural scientist cannot help, however, developing preferences, and mine lie in the direction of big, predatory, meat-eating creatures—like *Phlegmosaurus carbonensis*. This is why I bring up the mammal, for it's often forgotten that the mammal came into his own only *after* the dinosaur became extinct. When the dinosaur was active the mammal dared not emerge from his hole. He was a timid, hairy little creature—I speak now in layman's terms—who never mounted any sort of a challenge to the dinosaur's domination of the Mesozoic environment. The point is, if we keep a close eye on Fledge, we will observe an identical tactic being employed—in this case, calculated opportunism on the part of an innately devious inferior with inflated social aspirations.

I don't wish to pursue the analogy; suffice it to say that Fledge's game was a waiting game and, as I say, only by the small signs he made is it now apparent what he was about. One such sign I remember distinctly, for it came, oddly enough, at a moment of, for me, bitter professional disappointment.

The blow fell on one of those lovely crisp, clear mornings we enjoyed last autumn; and it fell, appropriately, in the barn. I had as usual eaten a good breakfast, spent half-an-hour in the lavatory with the *Times*, and made my way downstairs; and there, on the hall table, I found a letter from the Royal Society. I turned it over in my hands for a few seconds; I was seized with a powerful premonition that the news it contained would be bad. I tucked it into my pocket and crossed the driveway to the barn.

Now the barn, I should tell you, is structurally no different from any other barn in this part of Berkshire. A central area is bounded by four pairs of upright timbers, and it was in this space that I conducted my research. At the north end (the barn stands at right angles to the house, and faces east) a narrow flight of wooden steps leads to a gallery that extends down the west wall and along the south wall and forms a sort of loft I used for storage of bones. Small windows high in the gables permitted a few shafts of daylight to penetrate the gloom, and as I entered, and closed the door behind me, I noticed a small bird, a sparrow, fluttering among the rafters.

I stood for a few moments with my back to the door, without turning on the lights. Structurally, as I say, this was like any other Berkshire barn; functionally it was not. This barn, you see, had been converted into a working research laboratory, and as my eyes adjusted to the obscurity, so did the bony creature on which I had been working for a quarter of a century come dimly into view. It was *Phlegmosaurus* himself—my reconstruction of the entire skeleton.

He was not tall, as dinosaurs go, a little under seven feet, with a long tail jutting out behind and supported by an iron upright embedded in a block of concrete.

Birdlike best approximates the creature, I think, with his huge feet, comprising two long, multiply articulated toes and a third inner toe resembling an oversized claw with a thin, curved, sickle-shaped blade. The hind legs were long, the hipbones broad, and from the pelvic arch the pubis protruded like a sort of giant flat-headed hammer. The barrel-ribbed torso was short, as were the long-fingered forearms, and atop the neck the head of the beast was narrow and pointed and crammed with vicious, fanglike teeth, all set in sockets. I had fixed the jaws wide apart such that he seemed, in his upright, rearing position, to be snarling, roaring even, and when I first brought Victor Horn, my grandson, into the barn to see him, the poor child was frightened half to death! But it was to the hind legs that my eyes were most often drawn in this, the final stage of my research, to the great claw-toes, to the single-hinged ankles, each with a sharp spur of bone projecting from the back like a crocket; to the long shanks, strutted with exquisitely slender fibulae, and to the long stem of femur that fit so snugly into its socket in the hip. *Birdlike*, I say; those legs looked like the legs of a pheasant, an immense pheasant, a monster of a pheasant, and it was this startling resemblance that had first set me thinking about the dinosaur-bird connection, and the possibility of a kinship far more intimate than orthodox paleontology was then prepared to admit. Distant cousins, orthodox paleontology would consider them. Not me. For me, *Phlegmosaurus* was the patriarch, and the line of descent was direct. Yes, *Phlegmosaurus* was the father of the birds—and this of course was the subject of my lecture.

I pressed the switch beside the door. Fluorescent

tubes, suspended from the rafters, flickered to life, and my haunted ossuary metamorphosed into the laboratory of a working paleontologist. It was only then that I sat down in the white wicker chair that faced the beast and opened my letter from the Royal Society. The news, indeed, was bad.

At lunch I was silent and morose. "Sykes-Herring," I said, "has written to me." There were only the two of us at table, Cleo and Sidney having gone off on bicycles to take rubbings from gravestones near Pock. Harriet had been out in the garden, and the brisk autumn weather had brought a glow to her cheeks. Her hair was gathered and pinned rather higher on her skull than usual, and she was gazing out of the window, giving me her profile, her nose slightly uptipped, her buttonlike chin couched snugly in the warm swell of flesh that had once been her neck. Her brow furrowed as she turned to me. "Now tell me again, dear, which one Sykes-Herring is, I get them all mixed up. Is he the pterodactyl man?"

"No, Harriet," I said, trying to keep the snappish tone out of my voice. "He's the Secretary of the Royal Society."

"Oh *yes*," she said. "Rather a sweet little man."

"Sweet or not," I said dryly, "he doesn't want me to give my lecture."

Harriet was indignant. "Not give your lecture?" she cried. "What, *never*?"

"He doesn't say. Apparently he's having trouble with the scheduling; I am to contact him at my earliest convenience."

"Well," said Harriet crossly, "I think that's perfectly dreadful of him. Now you'll be impossible all winter."

I frowned. This was not what I wished to hear, not at all. Impossible indeed! Harriet, I think, realized her gaffe, and nervously touched her hair. A sort of cough came from Fledge. A sudden gust rattled the window-panes, and was followed by a brisk volley of rain. Harriet turned toward the window again and said, distractedly, "Oh dear, Cleo and Sidney will be quite soaked." I glanced at Fledge, and I saw it: he was covering his mouth with his hand. He was doing this, I am convinced, not to muffle a cough, but to conceal the fact that *he was laughing at me*.

I have thought long and hard about that gesture of Fledge's, for it was the first real indication I had that the man was not what he seemed; and yes, he was laughing at me. He found me absurd. He thought it ridiculous, clearly, that I should angle for my wife's sympathy and then allow myself to be slighted as I had. I daresay he was right—but I was damned if I'd let him laugh in my face like that! I could hardly confront him with it, however; it was all too easy to imagine his cool "Sir?", his cool "I beg your pardon, Sir Hugo?" I would merely compound my absurdity, my humiliation, in his eyes.

I returned to the barn in a foul, black mood, a mood that grew fouler and blacker all afternoon, as, indeed, did the weather. I stopped working on the leg at about three, and had a large scotch. I was of course furious with the Royal Society, and with Sykes-Herring in particular, for obstructing me, for putting obstacles in my path. But this was not new; my relationship with the paleontological establishment had never been cordial, for I was no orthodox paleontologist, I was no *house* paleontologist, like Sykes-Herring and his ilk. No, this was a familiar conflict. What did raise my hackles was the lack of sympathy I found in Crook. Harriet was more concerned about this alleged "impossibility" of mine than she was about Sykes-Herring's machinations, and my own butler laughed at me to my face! I went back to the house at six, and learned that Sidney and Cleo had come home wet and miserable a half-hour previously and been packed off by Harriet to have hot baths. This is always a perilous undertaking in Crook, given the state of the plumbing, but whatever household gods are responsible for pipes, boilers, etc., that day, apparently, they were smiling.

I, however, was not smiling. I sat on the edge of my bed, over in the east wing, in my socks and underwear, and I seethed. I had brought a large scotch up with me; I was smoking a cigar. There came a light tap on the door. "Come!" I barked. It was Mrs. Fledge. She had brought me a clean shirt. "Oh excuse me, Sir Hugo," she whispered, and made as if to withdraw.

"Come in, come in!" I shouted. "Never seen a man in his underpants, Mrs.Fledge? Just hang it on the back of the chair, will you."

She scurried across the bedroom with eyes downcast. What a timid creature she was—had Fledge reduced her to this, with his chilly, sardonic ways? "Mrs. Fledge!" I said. Having hung up my shirt, she was halfway to the door. She froze, and stood there, her eyes averted from me, her back slightly stooped, her shoulders pulled in toward her flat bosom, a tall, workworn woman with a tight bun on the back of her head and a beaky, red-tipped nose. Her long white hands drooped limply from the wrists, red and rough about the knuckles, I noticed, from all the washing she did. She would not look at me. I clamped the cigar between my teeth, rose to my feet, and began to put on my clean shirt. "Mrs. Fledge," I said, "what do you think of me?"

"Oh Sir Hugo," she murmured, casting at me one quick furtive sideways glance, "that's not for me to say."

"No, come, Mrs. Fledge," I said, buttoning the shirt, "do you think, for instance, that I am an *impossible* man?"

"Oh not a bit, Sir Hugo," she said, with apparent sincerity. This was something, at any rate.

"You don't find me impossible?" I said. "You find me—reasonable?"

"Yes, Sir Hugo."

"Am I absurd to you, Mrs. Fledge?"

"No, Sir Hugo."

"Not absurd? Not impossible? A perfectly decent, reasonable, straightforward man?"

"Yes, Sir Hugo."

"I wonder, Mrs. Fledge, if you would mind fastening my cuff links for me."

I sat on the edge of the bed and she leaned over me, fastening my cuff links with her long thin washerwoman's fingers. She smelled of carbolic soap, but not of sherry—on the wagon, perhaps. "Mrs. Fledge," I said. I was gazing at the top of her skull, as she bent over me, examining her silver-threaded hair. "Mrs. Fledge, I wanted to ask you about your husband's sense of humor."

"I beg your pardon, Sir Hugo?" she murmured faintly. Her fingertips brushed my left wrist.

"Fledge's sense of humor. Does he like a joke? A prank? A bit of fun?"

"Not so as you'd notice, Sir Hugo."

"Laughter does not come easily to him, Mrs. Fledge?" I said.

She lifted her head then, and looked me straight in the eye. She twitched her nose and sniffed. Then she dropped her head once more, and busied herself with my right cuff. "We've not had much to laugh about, Fledge and I," she muttered.

"Is that so?" I said. I chewed my cigar, mulling this over. "A hard life, eh?"

"Hard enough, Sir Hugo."

"You knew hardship in Kenya?"

"Of a sort, Sir Hugo. There!" She stood up. "Will that be all, Sir Hugo? I've still the potatoes to see to."

"And what," I said, ignoring her evident desire to flee, "would amuse your husband, then, Mrs. Fledge?"

She had retreated to the door. "I'm sure I can't say, Sir Hugo. Excuse me!" And she was out of the door, leaving only a faint whiff of carbolic behind her. I rather like the smell of carbolic; it reminds me of my own days in Africa.

My little chat with Mrs. Fledge cheered me, in some curious way, and when I descended the stairs, dressed for dinner, some fifteen minutes later, I was feeling a good deal more jaunty than I had all day. Not that I intended to demonstrate this; there were still scores to settle, with Harriet and with Fledge, and I did not intend that this should be a happy evening in Crook. I reached the drawing room to find Harriet asking Sidney whether his bath had been hot enough. Sidney was always animated when he talked to Harriet. "Oh yes, Lady Coal," he cried—he was sitting on the edge of the couch, beside Cleo, the pair of them like some latter-day Hansel and Gretel—"oh, it was as hot as I could bear it! And I sat there so long I came out wrinkled like a prune and pink as a lobster!"

I suppressed a savage snort of rage that an inanity like this should be uttered in my own drawing room. Harriet smiled anxiously at the young couple. "I do hope you didn't catch colds?" she said.

Cleo was drinking a large gin. She drinks heavily for a girl her age—my fault, I'm afraid, she takes after me. "Well I don't think you look like a lobster," she said.

Sidney turned to her. They were sitting very close together on the couch—it was Cleo's proximity that permitted him to express himself so freely, despite my glowering, terrifying presence. His soft baby's skin grew puckered with silliness. "Oh you don't!" he said, with a shrill laugh.

"No," declared Cleo, "I think you look more like a ferret."

"A ferret!" he screamed, and the pair of them dissolved in giggles.

Harriet smiled indulgently. "A ferret," she said. "Oh no, darling, Sidney doesn't look at all like a ferret. I should say Sidney looked like—an otter. Yes, an otter."

As this fascinating conversation went forward Fledge appeared and announced that dinner was served.

I AM NOT, as you will have observed, a man greatly enamored of his fellow human beings. I do not enter lightly into the foibles and whimsicalities of others, I do not suffer fools gladly, I seem able, in conversation, only to needle or be needled. My relationships, as a result, are few, and those few are tenuous, prickly sorts of arrangements, altogether lacking in the spontaneity and intimacy for which humans, I'm told, have an instinctive need. I am aware of no such instincts in myself. But there is a type of dour and taciturn individual in whose company I can, I find, be at ease—men with strong, uncomplicated natures and no interest in chatter. Silent, solid men. My gardener, George Lecky, was just such a man, and it is high time, I think, after listening to Sidney's fatuous nonsense, and witnessing the furtive mockery of Fledge, that you were introduced to him.

One morning, shortly after the Sykes-Herring letter, unable to work, I left the barn and set off briskly down the road to Ceck. This was not a thing my doctor recommended, on account of my sclerotic coronary arteries, but it was something I used to do anyway, as nothing gave me more pleasure than a brisk walk in the country round Crook. Sadly, I had no dog with me— my old setter Wallace had died during the summer, and I hadn't had the heart yet to replace him. Well, the sky was blue, with squadrons of big, thick white clouds blustering across it, and the air was rank with the good strong smell of manure, and of fallen leaves just beginning to rot. The fresh-turned soil in the fields beside the road contributed its own rich odors to the day, and there were still, I noticed, a number of birds about, swallows and martins for the most part, and of course the crows that stay with us year round; a group of them were assembled on the roof of the Hodge and Purlet, and as I approached the pub they set up a raucous chorus of derisive caws.

The Hodge and Purlet is an old establishment, almost as old as Crook itself, and it shows its age. The ceilings are low, the floors uneven, and the framing timbers that stand out so blackly against the white-plastered walls are riddled with deathwatch beetle. But while Crook is built on high ground, the Hodge and Purlet stands not far from the marsh, and the dampness of the earth beneath has for centuries been seeping up through the cracks in the flagged stone floors such that the building has a faintly greenish tinge to it today, caused by tiny fungoid colonies that, despite being constantly scrubbed off, always come creeping back. As for the name, *hodge* derives from an Old Dutch word for mutton stew, and *purlet* refers to a chain of twisted loops such as might once have been embroidered on the edge of a piece of lace, or inlaid in the border of a violin. Accordingly, upon the weathered sign that hung over the door of the inn was painted a steaming stewpot within a faded circle of interlinked, oval-shaped loops. This wordless sign was gently creaking on its rusty chains as I passed beneath it and entered the public bar, seeking the solace of men with strong, uncomplicated natures. Shortly before noon George appeared, accompanied by old John Crowthorne, who helped him with the pigs.

George was a big man, and he had to bend his head to get through the door. Then, straightening up, he cast his eye over the room and, finding it occupied only by myself, he suddenly opened wide his jaws and displayed a set of large, square, yellowing, horselike teeth. Now George, I should tell you, was a man of extremely few words. But he did possess a deep and subtle intelligence—a sort of wisdom, in fact, a countryman's wisdom—and many years ago, in Africa, where I met him, I had learned to watch his gestures, if I wished to know his meaning, and the fleeting expressions that touched his long-jawed, horsey face, rather than listen to his words, which were, as I say, rare and brief. It was only through this mute, muscular vocabulary of gesture and expression that one could ever know what George was thinking. The drawing back of the lips from the teeth that I have just described—a most peculiar and un-

36

sightly rictus—the meaning of that, however, the emotion it was intended to express, I had never been able to fathom. It certainly wasn't a smile; simply, it was something George *did* in situations that seemed to call for it. I took it for a greeting in this context, and waved gaily at him as he took off his cap, rubbed his cropped and nubbled skull with a huge, grimy hand, and then patted the pockets of his old, frayed, pin-striped jacket, looking for his pipe.

A big man, I've said; and there was not an ounce of fat on him, he was as lean and strong today as he had been when I'd first met him, more than twenty-five years before. He had thick black eyebrows that meshed in a heavy hedge at the root of his nose, and he wore old brown corduroy trousers tied at the ankles, above big muddy boots, with string; and having found his pipe, he advanced into the room, smelling of pigs and earth and twinkling with a sort of dry, laconic irony that was habitual with him and a true reflection of his nature. Old John Crowthorne, a local man, was already at the bar and had bid me a good morning; he too smelled strongly of pigs. I paid for their pints and began to regain my good humor. With men like these I could forget Sykes-Herring and his petty machinations, I could forget the simpering Sidney, and the scheming Fledge.

Well, we stood there at the bar, and the light of that brisk autumn day came drifting in through the little windows and fell in irregular splotches and puddles on the old worn gray flagstones that still bore the scratches where, in the old days, they'd been nightly chalked to keep out the witches. A good fire was burning in the grate, and our talk was of pigs, and the weather, and

the land, and such, and it came in sporadic bursts, all
in that rich, slurry Berkshire dialect I'd picked up as a
boy, and could still fall into at times like this; and in
the silences George would charge his great black pipe
with shag, and old John would whistle between his
toothless gums as his bright, restless old eyes darted
about the place, as if he were searching for some lost
object. Harbottle, the landlord, in a white apron as vast
as a mainsail, leaned on the bar and murmured scraps
of the Ceck gossip to us.

It gives me pain to think about him now, poor
George, for he was not a bad man, and I can see him
still, so clearly, standing there at the bar beside me,
quietly smoking his pipe, a pint of brown ale before
him, and occasionally lifting his leg to stamp a hob-
nailed boot on the stone floor with a great ringing
sound. The sunlight shafted across his body in a thick,
yellowy stripe, and along its beam, faintly buzzing,
drifted a languid wasp, last survivor of the summer, just
emerged, perhaps, from a basket of wrinkled apples
that stood neglected in a little window alcove on the far
side of the room. It crawled across the bar toward a
pool of spilt beer and George, who had been gazing
absently into some middle distance of his memory, suddenly took notice of the creature. Placing a large thumb
into the pool of beer, he permitted the insect to crawl
onto his cracked, horny nail, then he lifted it into the
light. The yellow-striped bulb of the wasp's abdomen
twitched with a sort of sleepy reflex as it crawled up
the nail and onto the tip of George's thumb. For some
reason both old John and myself were gazing intently
at this silent drama. George then bared his teeth and,

placing his middle finger on the insect's thorax, very slowly crushed it to a pulp on the end of his thumb. Old John sniggered; I snorted once, myself, then lit a cigar and ordered more drinks as George wiped his hand on the seat of his trousers. The incident prompted me, I remember, to start talking about the insects of Africa; for it was in large part due to an infestation of flies in Tanganyika in 1926 that George and I had ever met.

It is no exaggeration, I think, to say that without George Lecky I would never have brought *Phlegmosaurus* back to Crook, and my contribution to British paleontology would have been nil. I was in Africa for the bones, of course; nor was mine by any means the first expedition to take the steamer from Dar es Salaam down to Lindi, that torpid, mosquito-ridden little hellhole on the Indian Ocean, just ten degrees below the equator. I don't wish to bore you with my African stories; suffice that when I learned that on account of the insects no donkeys or mules could be used for the trek inland to my prospective site—nor, more crucially, for bringing out the bones I planned to unearth there—my first impulse was to abort the expedition altogether. Then, a day or two later, as I sat morosely in a squalid little tin-roofed bar near the docks, drinking quinine and gin beneath a slowly turning ceiling fan that barely stirred the thick, dripping heat of the afternoon, a British soldier, recently discharged from the service, came to me and announced that he would recruit and supervise the native bearers I required. I hired him on the spot; it was George, of course.

It was a four-day tramp, in intense tropical heat, inland from Lindi to the range of hills in which I found my *Phlegmosaurus*. Into those hills we had to sink deep pits to get at the fossil-bearing strata, for the bones had not been exposed, as they are in cliffs and ravines when erosion has helped the paleontologist in his labors and scattered them about the landscape. How many times George made the grueling trip from the diggings to the coast and back, I cannot now remember. He was very tough. I do remember how, in the early morning, while the sun was still bearable, I would pause on the peak of a steep, grassy hill, and there, under the huge African sky, with tree-spotted plains stretching for miles on every side, I would watch George organize his bearers in the camp below. The small bones they carried in boxes on their heads; the heavy ones, the femurs and vertebrae, would be slung on poles, and each pole hoisted between the shoulders of two men. When they were ready George would gaze up the hill and, shielding his eyes from the sun, bare his teeth at me. I doffed my pith helmet and, from my grassy eminence, waved it at him; then off they would go, in a long, snaking line, across the plain towards the sea, chanting as they went. But I knew that in a week I would see them again, with letters from home, newspapers, and fresh supplies of chocolate, quinine, and brandy.

When it was all over, and enough bones had been shipped to England to keep me busy for a lifetime, I asked George to come back with me to Ceck, and run the pig farm. He'd spoken of his ambition to farm; I was only sorry, I said, that I couldn't offer him anything better.

* * *

John Crowthorne loved to hear me talk of those days. Though he must have heard the African stories on a hundred occasions, the romance and the exoticism seemed never to fade; he was like a child listening to its favorite fairy tale. George, though, simply sucked on the stem of his pipe, wearing his habitual, slightly amused air of fatalistic resignation. We emerged, some hours later, into the afternoon. The Hodge and Purlet faces the Ceck green, on the far side of which a few boys were kicking a football around. The day was hazy, the shadows had grown long, and the sun was now a molten ball as it sank behind a bank of gilded clouds, low in the reddening western sky. Upon the windows of the Hodge and Purlet bars of late sunshine gleamed like gold. Old John went off about his own affairs, and George and I walked slowly round to the yard, where he had parked his swill lorry. This was a filthy, dilapidated vehicle the back of which was crowded with the dustbins in which he twice weekly collected his swill, the scrapings and peelings of the Ceck kitchens, which, mixed with damp bran, fed the pigs. We stood there in the soft, misty light of that late September afternoon, mellowed by drink and memories, and as the good organic stink of his dustbins reached my nostrils, I said: "They were good days, George."

He was gazing out past the pub at the boys on the far side of the green, and doing some business with his pipe. He gave me one of those sardonic looks of his. I read the humor in his eyes, and though he said nothing I knew what he was thinking: the old days are *always* the good days—such is the nature of memory. How wise he was.

I MADE MY way back to Crook as the light thickened; and what a glorious dusk it was! For a mile or so I walked due west, and across a flat expanse of fields I watched the sky steadily deepen in color as the sun settled on the black wedge of the horizon, and then went down. The clouds had massed in a peculiar arrow-like formation, the tip of which seemed fastened to the sinking sun, so that they swept toward the horizon in two great converging wings, all in bitty, vaporous flecks that shifted through a layered spectrum from the pale pastel blues and grays of the upper strata through violets and purples to rich, sultry crimsons that merged almost imperceptibly with the blackness of the land. The smells were strong as ever, and spiked now with wood smoke, and in the middle distance reared a single stark dead

42

elm tree, its fingery, leafless limbs etched sharp and densely black against this vivid cloth of sky.

My road then swung round to the south and began gently to climb, and now I moved toward a darkened sky that bristled with trees, though still, to the west, the sunset continued quite gloriously to play itself out. I remember it all so distinctly because these were in a sense the last *good* days. Of course I was not aware of this at the time; at the time I was preoccupied, as you know, with my professional and domestic problems. Only now, in retrospect, do I see the true dimensions of those problems; for they were soon to be massively overshadowed, and the darkness that then entered my life was as dramatic in contrast to what went before as night is to day.

I plodded on through the dusk, and very elegiac my mood should have been, I suppose; but I was untouched, I confess, by mournful reflections on death and the dead. I was thinking, rather, about the birdlike characteristics of the hipbone and hind leg of the dinosaur. Even full of brandy and African memories, you see, even in the presence of that gorgeous sunset, my mind went slipping back to its single, all-consuming passion—the beast that bore my name, *P. carbonensis*.

The road wound gently up the hill toward Crook, and now I had trees on either side of me, and the descent of darkness was almost complete. The cries of birds, and the sudden scufflings of furtive woodland creatures, broke now and then into the stillness of this twilit world. For some minutes I permitted myself to become absorbed in a familiar fantasy, in which the civilization that encroached with increasing shrillness upon these quiet natural places simply vanished into thin air, and I moved upon a planet that knew nothing of humanity. How hard it is to lose the self! Almost impossible, to ditch that gibbering little monkey and merge for even a moment with the Nature of which we are a part, yet from which we have so effectively alienated ourselves. Drink helps; drink opens the receptive faculties, and as I climbed the hill to Crook I managed, for a minute or two, to attain some sort of primal, unmediated contact with the earth. Such experiences are rare and fleeting and now, for me, impossible of course. My next unmediated encounter with Nature will occur six feet under!

At last I reached the rusting, wrought-iron gates of Crook, so overgrown with grass and ivy that they would never again be closed; and so up the drive between the trees, the evening chorus of the birds raucous in my ears. Rounding the bend in the drive, I found Crook heaving up before me against a sky in which the last dim light still faintly lingered. Black against that darkling air, no line straight, it seemed a great, skirted creature that rose by sheer force of will to thrust its wavering gables at the sky—a foundering mastodon, it seemed, a dying mammoth, down on its knees but tossing its tusks against heaven in one last doomed flourish of revolt. In the windows downstairs the lights shone into the night, and thus did the life of the house still burn, still feebly burn, and then, only then, as I stood at the bend in the drive and leaned, panting, after my climb, on my walking stick, only then did I experience a sudden intimation of mortality: my house would go down as I would go down; we were the last of the line.

I had had my elegiac moment after all. In through the front door I came, suddenly very hungry indeed. There, on his hands and knees, halfway down the hall, was Sidney Giblet. Whatever was the fool up to? He turned his head toward me; he had been examining a section of decorative carving on the skirting board. "Sir Hugo," he cried, in tones of aesthetic fervor, "*what* a treasure!" Silly ass, I thought; and, glaring at his little bum, sticking into the air, I suppressed only with difficulty a powerful urge to give it a good kick.

THESE, AS I say, were the last of the good days, and I think often of them now, for I wonder if anything occurred then that might have warned me about what was to come. I was unaware at the time of Fledge's designs; I knew only that he displayed toward me a good deal less of the deferential respect than I had a right to expect from my butler, but of his *evil* I was still ignorant. And other than his presence, and Doris's, all was as usual in Ceck and environs. There was the business with Sykes-Herring, of course, but that was nothing new; I'd been warring with the Royal Society for years. I telephoned the man a day or so later and made an appointment to see him two weeks hence. He was smoothly affable to me, deeply regretted, so he claimed, the "unavoidable postponement" of my talk, treated me, in short, with the sort of patronizing smugness that the gentleman naturalists must expect from his "professional" colleague in these times. The problem is, men like Sykes-Herring, themselves blinkered, find the breadth of vision of a naturalist like myself acutely threatening, for, as a function of their long formal training, they are devoid of the most vital of scientific attributes, *imagination*. They bring too much categorical and theoretical baggage to the task, they see what they expect to see and no more. The gentleman naturalist, by contrast, has an open-minded and theoretically eclectic attitude toward natural phenomena, and is thus far better equipped for informed, imaginative speculation. He is far more likely to make the sudden brilliant intuitive leap to revolutionary truth. This is why I have always had such trouble with the Royal Society, with men like Sykes-Herring; this is why they accuse me of mixing up my bones, why they refuse to publish my papers, why they sabotage my lectures. They practice safe science, and safe science to my mind is no sort of science at all.

All this I had of course long been aware of. Nevertheless, Sykes-Herring's letter, and the animosity that lay behind it, disturbed my concentration, for I found myself during the days that followed unable to spend more than an hour or two at any one time with the bones. The whole business, my lifework, *Phlegmosaurus*: a sense of bitter futility impregnated all my thoughts, and I simply could not stay with it with any sort of zeal.

I spent many afternoons in the Hodge and Purlet during this period, but I don't want to give you the impression that I always returned to Crook in the wistful, elegiac mood I have just described. In fact, it was only on that one occasion it occurred, I believe, which is probably why I remember it. No, after a few hours in the public bar I tended to come home in a fractious, irritable state of mind; day drinking always makes me irritable, for some reason. I would look for trouble. I would pick on people (usually Sidney). I'm rather sorry, then, in the light of what happened, that on the notable evening that Sidney and Cleo announced their engagement I did not respond very graciously. This I regret not only because I hate at any time to give Cleo pain, but also because it was, for Sidney, one of the last moments of happiness he would know.

We always dress for dinner in Crook, and I prefer candlelight to electric light in the dining room. The meal thus tends to be an affair of rather gloomy formality (and this, frankly, is altogether to my taste). Fledge was striking the gong as I emerged from my bedroom in the east wing, and as I clattered down the stairs I heard Harriet and Sidney and Cleo leave the drawing room with a gush of giggles and excited whispering, and cross the hall to the dining room. What, I asked myself, are they all so happy about? Probably still discussing whether Sidney looked more like a ferret or a lobster.

Mrs. Fledge had made us one of her shepherd's pies. She makes a fine shepherd's pie, the meat bubbling gently in its own juices and the mashed potato on top whipped up like a choppy sea, its little crests crisply browned under the grill. All through soup (we had Heinz canned tomato soup) I'd been aware of a sort of suppressed giddiness in Sidney and Cleo—frequent glances across the table, grins and snorts and so on, and I knew something was afoot, though I was not particularly interested in what. Fledge served the shepherd's pie from the sideboard, and then came round the table with the runner beans; and barely had I washed down the first mouthful with a draft of burgundy than Harriet said: "Hugo."

Here it comes, I thought. "Yes?"

"Sidney has something to tell you, dear."

I glanced over at the boy, pushing a small mound of meat, potato, and runner bean onto the end of my fork as I did so. Even in this dimness I could see him blushing. His fingers—Sidney had rather long, thin fingers—fluttered to his horn-rims, then touched his hair, which was combed sleekly back from his forehead and oiled so heavily that it gleamed in the flickering candlelight (it was this sleekness, I presume, that had provoked all the ferret-and-otter nonsense). He looked across at Cleo and tittered. "One feels so silly," he said. "You tell him, darling!"

Cleo had her arms flat on the table and was leaning forward toward the boy, grinning. Her eyes were alight. She shook her head slightly and said nothing. She was enjoying his embarrassment.

"Come on, Sidney," I said, dabbing at my lips with my napkin and swallowing more burgundy, "spit it out."

"Yes, Sidney," said Cleo, "spit it out."

He controlled the wave of hysteria that this remark evidently provoked. "Cleo and I," he began; and then, turning to Harriet: "Oh I can't, Lady Coal, I simply can't!"

"What Sidney is trying to say," said Harriet, "is that—"

"That Cleo and I want to be married!"

I allowed a small silence to occur. "You do," I said at last.

"Yes, Sir Hugo," he said, gazing at me now with an expression of great earnestness and trying not to look at Cleo. "Not immediately, of course, we can't afford to, immediately, but we should like, that is, with your blessing, of course, to, ah, announce our engagement." Then he permitted his eyes to drift back across the table to Cleo's, and the pair of them grinned at each other in the candlelight, and he stretched out a fluttery hand and laid it upon hers. Harriet gazed at me with a sort of expectant complacency, but I was concentrating on the assembly of neat forkfuls of meat, potato, and runner bean, each followed by a swallow of burgundy. They all awaited my response. Fledge loomed over by the sideboard, still and impassive in the shadows. I lifted my glass and the candle flames caught the crystal facets and darted off in all directions in thin sharp glinty spears of light. Fledge floated over with the decanter and refilled me. I was thinking of the evening I proposed to Harriet. I had had to go to her father, the colonel— Herbert—in his study after dinner, and quite an ordeal it was too. The old man had questioned me briskly about my prospects, and afterwards we had smoked cigars and talked blue-chip stocks by the fire. Apparently one didn't go about it like that anymore; apparently one now did it over dinner, in front of the servants, with grins and giggles. And to this piece of levity I was expected to give my blessing; Harriet clearly expected this; I'd have thought she knew me better than that.

My eyes were on my plate; my knife and fork were busy. "Prospects?" I murmured, without looking up.

"I beg your pardon, Sir Hugo?" Sidney's hand fluttered off Cleo's and dabbed at his spectacles, then at his hair.

I lifted my head, raised my eyebrows, and said again, quite mildly: "Prospects. What are your prospects, Sidney?"

"Oh darling, I hardly think we need go into that now," said Harriet, suddenly sensing danger.

"On the contrary," I said. "Sidney apparently considers the dinner table a fit place to ask for my daughter's hand; I consider it no less fit to ask him how he proposes to support her."

"Oh don't be stuffy, Daddy," said Cleo. "We want to celebrate."

I turned upon the girl. "I am not being, as you put it, stuffy. I am asking a perfectly reasonable question. I am asking how Sidney intends to support you."

"We'll muddle along," said Cleo blithely, "just like everybody else does."

I was suddenly struck with the notion of telling the colonel, all those years ago, that Harriet and I intended to "muddle along." Ha!

"I have my job in the bookshop," said Sidney, "and when I've learned the business I should like to open a bookshop of my own."

"What with?" I said, as I consumed the last of my shepherd's pie. It really was very good.

"I beg your pardon?"

"What with!" I cried, reaching for my wine. "Where will you get the money? Save it from your clerk's salary?"

"My mother said she might help me," said Sidney.

"She might!"

"Oh Daddy, stop being so awful. You're deliberately being difficult. I shall work too."

"What as, may I ask?"

"Oh, I don't know. I'll find something or other."

"Something or other," I said dryly. It was at that moment that I noticed Fledge leaning over to whisper something to Harriet. What new conspiracy was this?

"Darling," said Harriet, gazing down at the table at me as Fledge quietly left the room, "can we talk about this later? Mrs. Fledge has made something special."

"By all means," I snapped. "Perhaps," I said, glancing at Cleo, "we won't be quite so vague later."

"Oh Daddy."

"Don't 'Oh Daddy' me, young woman! I'm perfectly serious; you'll have to be a good deal more realistic about the future if you want my consent to any of this. You do still intend to go up to Oxford in October, I take it?"

But before we could get into the Oxford question—Cleo was to read philosophy at St. Anne's, and I was not going to permit her to jeopardize *that*—Fledge opened the door, then stood aside to let his wife come in. She was bearing a large white cake on the top of which, in some sort of horrible pink paste, had been drawn a rather wobbly heart, and an arrow, and, intertwined among them, the names of the lovers. Cleo let out a large snort of mirth and rose to her feet. "Bravo, Mrs. Fledge!" she shouted, lifting her wineglass. "What a creation!"

Mrs. Fledge set the cake on the table with a small simper and then stood back, absently drying her hands on her apron. She appeared slightly glazed, and her hair was unkempt, as usual. I lit a cigar and kept my eye on her, as Sidney and Harriet made noises of awe and wonder over her revolting confection. I presume all this was in honor of the "engagement." Fledge came forward with a knife, and as he began to cut the cake Mrs. Fledge sniffed once or twice, then produced from her sleeve a small handkerchief, and blew her nose. She brushed a tear from her eye—I had not yet realized how easily she succumbed to weepy emotion—and only then did she become aware of my gaze upon her. With my teeth clenched about my cigar, my chin resting on my interlocked fingers, and my eyes narrowed, I stared at her across the candlelit table, and she, for a moment, through damply shining eyes, quite boldly answered my stare. What a queer bird she is, I thought, as she grew suddenly frightened, and her eyes darted away. I could pursue my reflections no further, as Harriet was attempting to press upon me a slice of cake; I had to employ considerable forcefulness to avoid being given a piece of the thing.

The weather grew very wild shortly after dinner, and I remember retiring to my study to do some work on the lecture. I couldn't seem to concentrate; the wind was howling about the house and hurling sheets of rain at the windows, and it unsettled me. I remember ringing for Fledge, as I couldn't locate any whisky for some reason, but the bloody man didn't appear. Eventually I went storming down the hallway to the kitchen. The lights had not been lit; a single candle threw a dim glow over a long figure reclining in a chair by the stove. "Fledge!" I cried, with some passion. "Didn't you hear me ring? Why didn't you come to me?"

The figure stirred—it was not Fledge, I realized, but his wife. "Oh Sir Hugo," she mumbled, "I do beg your pardon. I must have dropped off!"

"Where is your husband, Mrs. Fledge?" I demanded to know.

"I believe he's upstairs, Sir Hugo, with Mr. Sidney."

"Upstairs with Mr. Sidney? What on earth is he doing upstairs with Mr. Sidney?" This information for some reason inflamed my irritation to the point of downright fury. What was he doing upstairs with Mr. Sidney? He was *my* butler, damnit!

"I'm sure I can't say, Sir Hugo," whispered Mrs. Fledge, sitting bolt upright in her chair and gazing at me with terrified eyes. "Is there something I can do for you?"

"Eh? Eh?" I glared at her as I tried to bring myself under control. "No, never mind, Mrs. Fledge," I said, after a moment or two, "I'll get it myself." And I strode out of the kitchen, still bristling, quite unaccountably, with rage, and went to look for whisky.

That night I had the strangest dream. Much of it is lost now, but what little remains is so startlingly bizarre I presume it is the core or meat of the dream, if a dream can be said to have meat. There were, to begin with, the sounds of a storm, and these I imagine permeated my sleeping mind directly from the night itself. The wind was wailing with a dreadful keening sound, and branches of trees lashed at the windowpanes while somewhere nearby the unlatched door of an outhouse kept banging relentlessly on its hinges. There was a howling, too, that was charged with the most profound misery imaginable, and all these wailings and howlings and lashings seemed magnified, both in volume and intensity, to such an extent that I felt, in the dream, confined and pressed in upon by them, and physically endangered. I was in a darkened room; it had features both of the public bar of the Hodge and Purlet—most vividly an uncurtained window filled with the moon— and of the drawing room at Crook. For I knew, somehow, that I sat, in the darkness, in one of the leather armchairs by the fireplace, which in the dream was a black, empty hole, a void, a nothingness. There were other people in the room, and scraps of talk, none of which I remember; my overwhelming sensation was one of fear, but also of great frustration, the frustration, I think, of being unable to move away from the source of the fear, which I identified simply as "outside." I gazed at the moon, and something went rapidly and furtively past the window, a sort of nude, hairy, red-brown thing with the head of a fox and the body of a man. And then I saw a figure kneeling on the rug before me, staring into the emptiness of the fireplace. I leaned forward and turned the face to mine: it was Mrs. Fledge. Lifting her chin with my fingertips, I kissed her mouth; and then I was overcome with sexual desire.

Somehow I got myself out of the armchair and onto

the rug beside her. I remember that she still smelled of carbolic soap. I put my hand under her apron and ran it up her stockinged thigh. She grinned at me in a sort of lewd, hungry manner quite foreign to the real Mrs. Fledge. I took hold of her underpants—they were men's underpants, oddly enough, like my own—and tried to pull them down. She said something indistinct in a curiously deep voice, then sat up and unfastened her suspenders. Then she lay back on the rug again, and, lifting her bottom, permitted me to slide her underpants off. She pulled up her apron, and the moonlight glowed on the white skin at the tops of her thighs, though the valley between them was black with shadow.

This now becomes the strange part of the dream, though maybe, to those who study such things, it is perfectly commonplace, perfectly banal. You see, I remember scrambling to my feet, and pulling off my overcoat, and then my jacket, and then my waistcoat, so that I could get at my braces, and push them off my shoulders, and get my trousers down; and as I struggled with these operations—they seemed never to end—I was feeling the most furious urgency to take advantage of this woman who was offering herself so frankly to me. I unbuttoned my trousers—I was wearing my winter suit, the heavy tweeds—and pushed them down. My penis—I am being very candid with you now—was, in the dream, quite stiff, and I daresay it was stiff also in the reality of my bed in the east wing of Crook, and it sprang forward through the buttons of my underpants and stood up at a steep angle, throbbing. Doris had meanwhile risen from the floor and was propped against one of the carved oak pillars flanking the empty fireplace, her back arched such that the moonlight gleamed upon the shiny material of her apron. I began to shuffle forward, though the tweeds about my ankles were heavily constricting. Doris's hands hung down by her sides and reminded me of a pair of long, pale, dead fish.

There was by now a wailing and howling outside the house fit to wake the dead, and the outhouse door kept banging, banging, banging on its hinges. Mrs. Fledge turned her back to me and, lifting her apron once more, offered me her bottom; the expression on her face, as she grinned at me over her shoulder, was one of quite brazen sexual invitation. But the trousers at my ankles by this time prevented me from going forward at all! I seem to remember that I groped at her with outstretched arms, but I simply *could not move*! The feeling of urgent, cruelly blocked desire became almost intolerable—doubtless I was suffering, physiologically, and at precisely the same moment, in my bed. And then, from *inside* the room, I heard a cough, and I turned, my arms still outstretched before me, toward the door. There, to my horror, stood Fledge.

I sat up in bed with a shout. The storm still raged; my head was pounding and my mouth was painfully dry. I no longer had an erection; there was, however, a small stain of discharged semen on my sheets. I poured a glass of water from the jug on my bedside table, as my head spun crazily in the aftermath of this dreadful dream, this nightmare. The strange thing was, you see, that I had not experienced sexual desire for—well, for a good many years.

* * *

The storm began to die down shortly afterwards, and by the time I arose the next morning it was a mere ghost of itself, a stiff breeze, I saw from my window, picking and ruffling through the boughs it had brought down in the night. The sky had a pale, washed-out aspect, a few high, white clouds drifting across it, fleecy, elongated things. The day seemed already exhausted, emptied of vigor, as it gazed upon the evidence of its nocturnal excesses; it mirrored my own mood exactly. There is a very comfortable white wicker chair in the barn, and it was in that chair that I used to sit when I wanted to mull things over quietly. Into that chair I now sank, having avoided the dining room entirely, and as my eyes played wearily over the familiar bones (I had not turned on the lights) and came finally to rest upon the spurred and gleaming leg of *Phlegmosaurus*, I attempted to shake off the very distasteful residue of that appalling dream. That it was purely and simply the effect of far too much whisky, a good deal of anger, and, quite probably, indigestion, I had no doubt, no doubt at all. But all the same, I had no little trouble regaining sufficient peace of mind to resume my work; I also had something of a hangover.

But slowly the bones reclaimed me, and in particular, the clawed toe on the foot of *Phlegmosaurus*, and the old, familiar question arose once more: what did a long, thin, sharply curved claw like that suggest about the creature that possessed it? There was only one answer possible: that as he went into the attack, he reared up on one leg to *slash* with it. Oh, he was a ripper, my *Phlegmosaurus*, he was a big, fast, fierce, dynamic animal capable of delicate balance and complex maneuvering. Does this sound like a reptile to you?

There was one curious and not strictly relevant sequel to my nightmare that I think deserves mention, as it has some bearing on my relationship with Fledge. You see, when I went back to the house for lunch that day, and encountered him in the dining room, I was for a moment seized with a quite irrational feeling of shame—as though I had in reality offended him as I'd dreamed I had, and should either avoid him altogether or apologize profusely. I did neither, of course; I gave him my usual curt grunt and took my place at the head of the table. He himself was as composed and inscrutable as ever, and served my soup and poured my wine just as he always did. But while Harriet chattered away to Sidney and Cleo about the storm, I could not help throwing surreptitious glances at the man, as if to confirm to myself that I had in fact dreamed the whole thing.

AT THIS TIME I was no great believer in omens and auguries and so on (I was still an empiricist, of course), so I did not connect my dream with an incident in the butler's pantry that occurred just a few nights later, an incident which, now that I look back on it, is quite clearly of crucial importance to the foul eruption of violence that in one sense forms the very marrow of this story. It was many months before we learned exactly *what happened* out on the Ceck Marsh that terrible night, but even before it happened I knew that things were going badly wrong, that we were entering a state of disorder. At the time I did not, as I say, connect my dream with the butler's pantry incident—there was no reason why I should, after all—but when I link them now, hold them in my mind in tandem, as it were, it is all too clear to me that even before the violence occurred there existed in Crook what I can only call "corrupt energies"—and I need hardly spell out who the source of those energies was. In fact, it occurs to me now that perhaps right from the start Fledge was causing a sort of moral infection in those around him—without our even being aware of it! I wonder, for example, whether he was responsible for that disgusting dream. And in retrospect I rather think he was, though as I say, at the time I wasn't aware of it; and with regard to the incident in the butler's pantry, I held Sidney as much to blame for that, if not more so.

Let me describe it just as it happened. I had been working late in the barn, and when I returned to the house it was all in darkness but for a single light left burning in the porch. I came in through the front door and very quietly closed it behind me. Before I had taken a single step down the hall, I heard a noise: someone was coming down the stairs.

Now, close to the front door of Crook there is a small table on which the mail is placed, and above it, attached to a baseboard of pale oak, rears the head of a large stag with glassy eyes and a fine spread of antlers. Directly opposite the stag stands a grandfather clock, and into the shadow of this clock I tiptoed, and waited there as the footsteps descended the last flight. Why I did this I have no clear idea, for I certainly wasn't in the habit of hiding in my own house. Whoever it was, though, he was carrying a candle, for its feeble light preceded him, throwing a faint flickering glow into the darkness of the hallway. I peered round the side of the clock as the footstep reached the hall, and then abruptly stopped.

Standing, listening intently at the bottom of the stairs, was Sidney.

He was wearing a tightly belted silver-colored dressing gown of some silky material, and the candlelight gleamed and flashed upon it as he turned this way and that, apparently assuring himself that he was alone downstairs. His pale, oval face, lit from beneath by the candle flame, glowed in a faintly eerie manner, the smooth cheeks plump and yellow as moons. Having satisfied himself that no one was about, he then moved off, on fawn-colored slippers of a very soft leather, toward the kitchen.

Separating the front of the house—the family rooms—from the back, where the kitchen, larders, and sculleries are situated, is a green baize door. I tiptoed down the hall and opened this door a crack, expecting to see the boy going along the passage to the kitchen. But that passage was empty; the door to the butler's pantry, however, which gave off the passage into the east wing, was just closing; I heard the latch click softly, and then there was silence.

In Crook, as in many country houses, the butler's pantry is that room where the butler can perform such tasks as polishing the silverware and sorting the mail, and, more important, where he can enjoy an isolation and privacy denied his inferiors in the domestic hierarchy. Not that this had much meaning here, of course, where the inside staff comprised only Fledge himself and his wife. But Fledge not only used this room, he apparently also *lived* in it—this I'd ascertained with my own eyes when I'd gone into the place a few days before. One descended a flight of stone steps—the stone floor of the pantry was below ground level—to a long narrow room with store cupboards along each wall, in which various household supplies were kept, light bulbs, mousetraps, and so on. A narrow, tightly blanketed iron bed was pushed up against the end wall, and beside it stood a washstand with hairbrushes and shaving gear. Sandwiched between two high cupboards, and beneath a very small window that looked out onto the lane that ran round the side of the house, was a workbench with a shelf just above it from which hung a set of small tools. Everything was very neat and well-swept the afternoon I went in, hunting, I seem to remember, for toilet paper. Whatever did Sidney want here at the dead of night?

My curiosity now thoroughly aroused, I retraced my steps back down the hall and out of the front door. There was some cloud that night, but the moon, which was close to the full, shone brightly on the slates and chimneys of Crook's steep gables. The thick coat of ivy that furred the walls glinted with a silvery sheen as its thousand fronds stirred gently in the night breeze. I made my way silently round the side of the house, to the lane that gave onto the back yard. Halfway along, at the foot of the wall, a neat square of light spilled onto the cobblestones from a small window. This was the window over Fledge's workbench. I crept towards it, my heart now beating dangerously fast.

Just before I reached the window I got down onto my hands and knees. Advancing on all fours, I very cautiously peeped round the side of the window. The pantry was lit by a single lamp, standing on the workbench. In the center of the room Sidney was facing

63

Fledge such that I could see both of them quite clearly in profile. I had never really noticed before how tall Sidney was; he was the same height as Fledge, five foot eleven or more. He was talking with some animation, smiling frequently and gesturing with his right hand, in which he held his little rosewood pipe. His hair gleamed in the lamplight, as did the silky, silver material of his dressing gown; it glimmered in streaks when he moved his arm. Fledge was in his shirtsleeves with his arms folded across his chest. His face was heavily obscured by shadow, and it was impossible for me to make out his expression as he listened to Sidney. I changed position, I hunkered down on the balls of my feet, clutching the edge of the windowframe, trying to get a clearer view of Fledge's face. Suddenly he smiled—never before, nor since, come to think of it, have I seen Fledge smile—and opened his arms. The two men seemed then to lean toward one another, and it was at this crucial moment, my blood rushing in hot turmoil in my veins, that I lost my balance and sat back heavily on my bottom, my feet scrunching loudly on the cobblestones as I did so. Of course they would have heard me; in an instant I had flattened myself against the wall, and I clung there, not even breathing, like a lizard. Fortunately it was not a window that could be opened, and so I was not observed. But a moment later the curtain was drawn and the small square of light blotted out. I slipped back round to the front of the house, but I did not go in. Instead I returned to the barn, where I sat and drank several scotches, lit only by the stray moonbeams that drifted through the little windows high in the gables. There I sat in my wicker chair until I reckoned it safe to make for the east wing. I regained my bedroom without incident, but, deeply disturbed by what I'd seen, I did not fall asleep until the first light of dawn had crept over the marsh to the east. You see, as I'd fallen back from the window, I *think* I'd seen Sidney taking Fledge into his arms to kiss him—yes, my butler, damnit, in the arms of that spineless boy!

I NEED NOT tell you my attitude toward that sort of thing. Men had been sent down from Oxford for less, in my day. Frankly I find it distasteful to have to mention it at all—I needed those scotches in the barn, they calmed me. My first reaction was to try and determine who bore the major responsibility for the incident. Fledge was the older man, of course, but Sidney was his better, in terms of social class, and in the fleeting glimpse I'd had of them it was Sidney who seemed, so to speak, the "aggressive" party. But I soon realized it hardly mattered which of them was more to blame, for in the normal course of events they'd both have been on their way before breakfast. But there was a complication, and it was this that kept me awake till morning.

My daughter Cleo was a spirited girl of eighteen, and this relationship with Sidney was her first real sentimental attachment. I've always had something of a soft spot for Cleo, despite my disappointment that she wasn't a boy. Cleo's a true Coal, as I may have mentioned; small-boned and wiry, she has prominent front teeth and fears nothing, not even me. I remember how, when the girls were growing up, I would at times have the entire household trembling with terror, and a sort of ghastly, oppressed silence hung upon the place, an "atmosphere," as Harriet called it. Cleo, though, would quite boldly bait me, not in the least intimidated by my snapping, snarling ill-humor. You see, she stoutly maintained the belief that beneath this splenetic and ogreish exterior there beat a heart of gold, though this I imagine was something she had to do, the idea that her father was splenetic and ogreish all the way through being just too grim to contemplate. In fact, not only is my heart not made of gold, it isn't even made of sound organic tissue— the arteries are sclerotic, and will kill me in the end!

I admired the girl, you see. Though I never showed it, I was delighted that she refused to allow me to tyrannize over her. So while Harriet and Hilary, my elder daughter, a plump and rabbity little thing like her mother, crept around in a state of deep funk, Cleo sought ways to provoke in me an outburst of truly foul temper. Punishment didn't deter her—as I say, she did not know the meaning of fear, and I remember once, during the war, how she climbed onto the roof of Crook and stood at the peak of the very highest gable to wave at the Spitfire pilots. Harriet almost died of anxiety, and I was far from calm myself as I stood in the driveway at the front of the house shouting at the bloody girl to come down, then watching her sliding and jumping over those mossy old slates, and clambering down a rickety drainpipe, certain that at any moment she would plunge to her death.

Given my feelings for the girl, then, I felt less than sanguine about rudely shattering her first affair, sending Sidney off with my execrations ringing in his ears, and then having to explain to Cleo *why*. It could scar her for life, put her off men for good. Marriage was now completely out of the question, of course, but I wondered if the thing could not be *gently* broken up—say, after Sidney had returned to his mother's house in London, about ten days hence. There would be no sudden shock, that way, no brutal exposure of the girl to the fact of Sidney's tendencies; he would leave Crook, and then I would quietly and firmly indicate to him, in writing, that any further contact with the family was impossible. Cleo would doubtless strike up new friendships at Oxford, and with any luck it would all "blow over." As for Fledge, I would have to keep him on until Cleo had gone, in case he made a scene; but once the girl was safely off to Oxford he'd be let go. And without references, I might add. It occurred to me then to wonder what precisely had happened in Kenya, that the Fledges should appear in England without papers of any sort. I felt a fleeting tremor of unease as I remembered what Harriet had said about the planter who'd been trampled to death by his own ox. I should have paid more attention to that tremor of unease; but I was not, in those days, in the habit of giving credence to such ephemeral and ultimately untestable phenomena.

All this I worked out in the long hours of the night, first in the unlit barn, and then in my bed in the east wing. As you may imagine, I was not a happy man at breakfast the next morning. I found it impossible to meet the eye of either Sidney or Fledge, and it was, as I say, only for Cleo's sake that I suppressed the disgust I felt at being in the same room as they. What perhaps was most sickening was that business of the "engagement" a night or two previously. How right I had been to remain aloof and skeptical—what a shoddy travesty it had been, what a mockery, what an insult, not only to Cleo, but to Harriet and myself. Just thinking about it made my blood boil; it was as well I had the barn to escape to, for had I been compelled to spend much time under the same roof as those two inverts I might well have been unable to mask my feelings.

I spent most of the next two days in the barn, and I'm afraid I drank a good deal of whisky. I hadn't as yet said anything to Harriet; that, I thought, should wait until Sidney was out of the house and back in London, for I had no confidence that she could keep up a pretense of normality if she knew what I knew. She would become upset, she would upset Cleo, and there would be no peace for any of us; and despite my recent setback I still had to work on my lecture. Better for everybody, I thought, if I keep it to myself. Mealtimes were difficult, and it was all I could do to maintain a sort of surly unsociability. But surly unsociability was not uncommon with me, and Harriet and Cleo were not particularly alarmed. Just Hugo having one of his "moods," they thought. Just Hugo being "impossible." Ha!

My plan, then, was to stay out of the house as much as possible for the last week-and-a-half of Sidney's visit. But three nights after the incident in the pantry a sudden and dramatic development occurred. And it was then, I think, that it can all be said to have definitely *begun*.

I was in my study, quite late, writing, when there came a tapping at my door. It was Cleo. She came in and sank into an armchair by the fire. "Daddy," she said, "Sidney's not back yet."

I did not look up from my work. Sidney's whereabouts did not interest me, not in the very least. "It's been more than three hours," said Cleo. "He was just going into the village to post a letter."

A rather cruel insinuation sprang to my lips. I suppressed it. Instead I said: "Perhaps he's discussing poetry with Father Pin." This was the parish priest, a friend of Harriet's.

"It's not like him," she said, gazing into the fire. "He's always so punctual about everything." Her hair fell forward in a short thick black curtain so that, in profile, I could see only the tip of her nose and her protruding top lip.

"Yes," I said, "I imagine he is."

"Don't be horrid, Daddy."

"Horrid?"

"I know you don't think very much of Sidney," she said, "but that's because you don't know him very well. He's always so shy in front of you."

My pen ran across the page, amassing the familiar evidence, drawing the bold conclusions. I reject the official notion that the dinosaur was a reptile. I claim a new class, the *Dinosauria*, separate and distinct from the *Reptilia*, and I include within it the birds. Yes, I claim the birds as *living dinosaurs*.

"You intimidate him," said Cleo. "He's not combative, like you. He has a gentle nature."

This of course was why Sykes-Herring was trying to muzzle me.

"You think that's just weakness, but it's not. I like gentleness, Daddy. All women do."

The idea was not original with me, unfortunately; Victorian paleontologists like Owen and Huxley knew all about the birdness of dinosaurs, and vice versa, but the insight had somehow been lost.

"Daddy, can't we drive into the village and look for him?"

I screwed the top onto my fountain pen and gave her my full attention. "Very well," I said. "Go and put your coat on."

We drove slowly into Ceck. The moon was full, though intermittently obscured by ragged black rainclouds. I parked in the yard behind the Hodge and Purlet and went into the saloon bar, then the public bar, while Cleo waited in the car. But no one had seen Sidney, so we walked up the lane behind the inn, between high brick walls and spreading elms in which a restless wind was gently murmuring. Entering by the lych-gate, we followed the narrow path that led through the graveyard to the church, which stood out sharply against the night sky, flooded by moonlight that silvered the stonework and threw the belfry and lancets into slender blocks of darkness. High above the little steepled building black rainclouds still fled across the face of the moon. We passed through the graveyard in silence, passed the scattered, tilting headstones, whose shadows were linked in shifting arabesques by the delicate tracery of the foliage of the trees along the fence, and but for the stirring of the boughs, and of their shadows on the moon-bleached grass, all was still as death.

We went round to the back of the church to the priest's cottage, and knocked on the door. Patrick Pin had not seen Sidney. Hunched in the dark little entrance of his cottage, the fat priest tried hard to get us inside, but I refused. We retraced our steps to the car, then drove out to Ceck's Bottom, on the possibility that Sidney had gone to see George. Off to our left, over the marsh, the moon hung huge and low and yellow against the sky. I began, then, to form an idea of what might have happened to Sidney, though I said nothing to Cleo.

I parked in the yard, beside the swill lorry. George's farmhouse was a square, squat, yellowing structure, and this night it seemed to glow, somehow, with an eerily vivid and unwholesome luster. I pushed open the back door and shouted his name. There was no answer. We went in, and the wind, which had freshened considerably in the last few minutes, slammed the door behind us with a bang. The kitchen was empty. A naked bulb hung from a length of twisted cord in the middle of the room and shed a dull, harsh light on the few sticks of furniture, the flagstoned floor, the rusting stove with its tin chimney rising crookedly through a hole in the ceiling and rattling dully as the wind came gusting down. A first volley of rain beat up against the window, which was uncurtained, one smashed pane patched over with a piece of damp cardboard. "George!" I shouted, and again there was no answer. It was weirdly disturbing, and my scalp for a moment prickled with a vague sense of dread—his lorry was in the yard and the light was on, but where was the man himself? I told Cleo to wait in the kitchen while I went through the house; but all the rooms were empty. "He's not here," I told her as I came back into the kitchen. The rain was lashing the windows by this time, and we could hear the pigs grunting on the far side of the yard. There was suddenly an ugly noise overhead, and Cleo turned to me, her eyes bright with alarm. It was a raspy, grating, scraping sound, and it seemed to accelerate, and as it did so it grew thunderously loud—it was a slate, I realized, dislodged by the wind, sliding down the roof. A second later it shattered on the stones of the yard, just outside the kitchen door. "Let's go back," said Cleo, with a shiver. It was all very uncanny. We returned to Crook in silence.

We left the front door unlocked that night, and we left the lights on in the drawing room. But Sidney did not come back.

"I suppose," said Harriet at breakfast, "we should telephone his mother. Perhaps he's gone home."

"But why, Mummy?" said Cleo, looking up from her boiled egg, the shell of which she was listlessly tapping with the back of her spoon. "Why on earth would he go home without telling anyone?"

"I don't know, darling," said Harriet. "And please don't play with your egg." She threw up her hands. "I simply don't understand the boy, do you, Hugo?"

I was behind my *Times*. I lowered it briefly. "Frankly no," I said. "But you're right, Harriet. Mrs. Giblet should be telephoned. I think you should do it."

Harriet sighed. "Yes, I suppose I should."

"Do it now, Mummy," said Cleo. "I just hate all this not knowing."

Poor Cleo. I'd said I didn't understand why Sidney had not returned to Crook. In fact I'd begun to form a pretty good hypothesis. That it was connected to his dealings with Fledge, this, I think, was clear; and it was my opinion that Fledge had attempted to blackmail the boy. It would hardly be the first time, after all, that a servant had tried to extort money from a "gentleman" in such a situation. No, my guess was that Sidney, having no cash with which to pay off the man, and unable to explain to his mother or anybody else why he needed the cash, had decided that the only solution was simply to drop out of sight for a while. I was relieved, frankly; this spared me the rather odious task of breaking up the relationship, for by the time Sidney surfaced again Cleo would have lost all interest in him—and I didn't expect him to surface again for a long time. In retrospect, this assumption on my part merits a loud, ironic snort. As for Fledge, I would wait until Cleo had gone up to Oxford, and then I'd sack him, as planned.

There remained one rather annoying loose end to tie up, and that was Sidney's mother. Ever since Harriet had telephoned her the old woman had been calling us from London three times a day for news. As I had an appointment in the city at the end of the week, with Sykes-Herring, I agreed to go and see the woman. Not a task I relished, and I think you can understand why. How, after all, to tell the boy's mother that I was sure he was all right, without telling her *why* I thought so?

MRS. GIBLET OCCUPIED a house in Bloomsbury, not far from the British Museum. After keeping my appointment with Sykes-Herring, and then eating lunch at the home of my elder daughter, Hilary, I took a taxi there. The sun had abandoned its efforts to bring light to the sordid metropolis, and retreated behind a thick mass of gray cloud. The weather served only to accentuate the aura of faded gentility that clung to Mrs. Giblet's street, which in turn deepened my own ill-humor, for I hate London. The knocker was a snarling griffin in tarnished brass; it provoked the shrill yap of a dog and a sort of muffled shuffling within. The door opened a crack and a timid face peered out. "Good afternoon," I said. "I believe Mrs. Giblet is expecting me."

The door opened a further crack to reveal a mousy

girl in a housemaid's uniform from the 1920s with a feather duster clutched in her paw.

"Who is it, Mary?" cried a raspy voice from the upper regions.

The mouse peered at me in terror. "Sir Hugo Coal," I said.

"Sir Hugo Coal!" she cried, surprisingly lustily.

"Who?"

"Sir Hugo Coal!" I shouted. "It's about Sidney."

"Show him into the parlor," came the voice. *"I'm coming down."*

I was then relieved of hat and coat and led down a narrow hallway, heavily carpeted, between walls crammed with sepia-toned photographs of young men in uniform and sour-looking family groups clustered in gardens. Various pieces of huge dark furniture constricted the passage, and the place smelled of boiled fish. I was shown into the parlor, where the gloom of that overcast day was filtered through windows curtained in dingy lace.

"Mrs. Giblet will be with you shortly," said the mouse, unnecessarily, and flicked her duster at a dead clock squatting massively on the mantelpiece. I removed a hank of animal hair from an overstuffed armchair and sat down. The air was musty, and whatever natural light did manage to penetrate the room was promptly swallowed by the unrelieved somberness of the hangings and furniture.

Some minutes passed; for me they were not happy minutes. I glanced at my watch. Nothing, I told myself, would keep me from the 3:47.

At last Mrs. Giblet appeared, leaning on a stick and

clutching to her bosom a silky-haired, pug-nosed lap-dog. The creature fixed me with an alert and hostile stare as I rose to my feet. With barely a glance at me, Mrs. Giblet made her way to a wing chair. Lowering herself ponderously into its depths, she wheezed heavily for several moments and regarded me from rheumy, china-blue eyes as her puckered lips worked over what I guessed were freshly inserted teeth. The voice, when it came, was rasping and steely and quite clearly accustomed to command. "Sherry, Sir Hugo? Or something stronger?"

"Sherry, if I may, Mrs. Giblet."

She nodded at the mouse, who scuttled away. Mrs. Giblet was what is popularly known as a battle-ax, a type I distinctly dislike (I knew several in Berkshire). Confirmed terrorists themselves, they are notoriously difficult to intimidate. Shrewd, too. She set her stick upright before her and folded her hands upon the handle. Her fingers were glittering with stones, the nails painted scarlet. Between their hooded flaps her eyes too were glittering. Her mouth was smeared with lipstick and her throat swung bagged and crosshatched from a wrinkled knob of chin flanked by rouged jowls loosely depending from lumpy cheekbones. Powerful gusts of stale scent emanated from the crannies of her person; the little dog was curled in her lap like a hairy tumor. The mouse returned with two glasses of sherry and was told to fetch the bottle. Mrs. Giblet fumbled in the depths of her clothing and produced a packet of Capstan Full Strength. "Cigarette, Sir Hugo?" she wheezed.

"Thank you," I said. There followed some business with matches and ashtray. When we were both alight, and the sherry bottle close to hand on a small round table with three clawed feet, I said, "Let me tell you what has happened."

"That would be a start," she said.

I sipped my sherry. It was very bad stuff. I frowned. "There isn't a great deal that you have not already heard from my wife," I began. "Sidney left our house on Monday evening at around seven o'clock, having told my daughter Cleo he was cycling into the village to post a letter to you."

Mrs. Giblet at this point lifted a hooked finger. "It is now Friday, Sir Hugo, and I have received no letter from Sidney. Even allowing for the idiosyncrasies of the Post Office, I think it would have come by now."

"Oh I agree, Mrs. Giblet. Clearly Sidney did not post the letter, if indeed there was a letter to post."

"You think," she said, with a rising inflection, "that Sidney had some other reason for going into the village?"

"I don't know, Mrs. Giblet. I think it possible. I've wondered if he might have had a reason for suddenly dropping out of sight?" I thought this would serve as an "opening."

"Such as what, Sir Hugo?" Her tone was very arch; apparently not.

"My dear Mrs. Giblet, I have no intention of casting aspersions on Sidney's character or motives. However, I find it hard to believe that some accident befell him; we should surely have found him if it had."

"No doubt. Please go on, Sir Hugo."

I was feeling distinctly nettled. I remained civil, however. "When he had not returned by ten, Cleo and

I drove into the village, but we found no sign of him. No one has reported seeing him that night, or subsequently. We telephoned the police the following morning. They have since begun a systematic search of the district.''

"Tell me please the name of the man in charge of the search for my son.''

"Limp," I said. "Inspector Limp.''

It did not inspire confidence. "Ah," she said. She pondered. There were deep bags under her eyes, semicircular flaps of rather bluish skin on which the years had etched delicate crow's-foot patterns. "And how does this—Limp—strike you, Sir Hugo?''

"He is not," I said, choosing my words with some care, "a very prepossessing character. Nevertheless, I've no reason to doubt his competence.'' In fact, Limp was about as stimulating as a bucket of water. But as I said, I had no reason to doubt he could mount a search for a missing person.

"I see. So Sidney remains lost in the countryside and a man called Limp is trying to find him. With dogs, Sir Hugo?''

"I believe so.''

"And what do *you* think has happened to him, Sir Hugo?''

"Mrs. Giblet, I may as well ask you the same question. I honestly have no idea. I'd thought at first that he might have got lost in the marsh.''

"The marsh?''

"The Ceck Marsh. It's dangerous in spots—boggy.''

"I see.''

"But then of course we'd have found him by now.''

"Not if he's been swallowed by one of your bogs, presumably." The idea did not appear to distress her unduly.

"In that case we should have found his bicycle."

"Perhaps he went down with his bicycle?" Those filmy old eyes glittered at me from under their hoods. The old bat seemed to be positively relishing this.

"That seems unlikely," I said.

"Which is why, Sir Hugo, you think Sidney has gone off somewhere of his own volition."

"It's possible, Mrs. Giblet, I say no more than that."

"But why would he do such a thing, Sir Hugo?"

"I thought you might be able to answer that, Mrs. Giblet."

"I have no idea."

"No more do I."

"Ah."

We had been staring straight at one another during this exchange. The old woman was utterly insensitive to my hints. I would have liked to speak frankly, but she wasn't making it easy. Now she dropped her eyes, and leaving her cigarette to dangle loosely from the corner of her mouth, clamped both hands atop her stick—into the crook of which, I now noticed, was set a tiny white skull, carved from a piece of ivory. Again she fell to pondering. I glanced at my watch. I would have to leave in five minutes if I was going to catch the 3:47. "And his bicycle?" she said at length. "They haven't found his bicycle?"

"No sign of the bicycle," I said.

"That's bad," she murmured.

"On the contrary, Mrs. Giblet," I replied, "that's

good. You see, I'm quite sure that Sidney is safe, and will come forward very shortly and clear up this distressing mystery." This at least was honest. "In the meantime"—I rose to my feet—"Inspector Limp has assured us that his description is being circulated to every police station and hospital in the Home Counties."

There was another long silence from the old woman. She heaved a deep sigh, her great bosom rose once, then fell, and those rheumy blue eyes flickered to mine. Wordlessly she picked a small bell from the table and shook it violently. The mouse appeared and helped her to rise from her chair. "Sir Hugo," she said, extending a hook, "so good of you to come and see me. Excuse me if I've been short with you—a mother's anxiety, I'm sure you understand"—and her whole face, the entire complex structure of flaps and jowls, heaved upward like a hulk being lifted from deep water and hung, trembling, for a moment, in an expression of genuine charm, before settling once more to its habitual aspect of irascible gloom. What a fierce old bird she was! I began to understand how Sidney had come by his tendencies. "Not at all, Mrs. Giblet. *Nil desperandum*, eh?"

"*Nil desperandum*, Sir Hugo," she said, taking my hand in hers and patting it once or twice. "Keep me informed."

"I shall."

I made the 3:47 with a minute to spare.

THERE IS SOMETHING I have learned
since being paralyzed, and that is that in the absence of
sensory information, *the imagination always tends to
the grotesque*. Fledge knows it too—this is why he turns
my wheelchair to the wall. He knows that when I sit
gazing at a panel of old oak, at its knots and whorls
and striations, and hear behind me only the murmur of
soft, muted voices, perhaps the rustle of silk, an intake
of breath, and even—from Harriet—a snort of mirth,
then the scene I construct will be one of venereal depravity, of sex in an armchair in the middle of the
afternoon.

This is what I mean when I speak of the grotesque—
the fanciful, the bizarre, the absurdly incongruous. For
when, on one occasion, Cleo entered the drawing room,
and with a cry of indignation turned my wheelchair

back around, I found the pair of them, Harriet and Fledge—playing chess! It thus becomes my task to *allow for* this tendency, to sift with rigorous care the circumscribed evidence of my senses, if I am to arrive at some approximation of the truth about what is happening in Crook. This, you will say, should not be difficult for a scientist such as I; but even for a scientist, pure empiricism is extremely hard to achieve, so hard, in fact, that one begins to doubt the possibility of constructing any version of reality that is not skewed in advance by the projections, denials, and impostures of the mind—or even (chilling thought) by a factor as simple and crude as the angle of vision afforded by the chance emplacement of one's wheelchair. Out of such accidents does "truth" emerge; I begin to think it a chimera.

I'm rambling. Sometimes it's an effort to keep everything in order. The reason is, that as I sit here brooding in my cave beneath the stairs, I suddenly detect fresh patterns of significance in the events that have occurred in Crook since the autumn, and these emerging patterns, if I'm not careful, play havoc with my chronology. This is unavoidable to a certain extent, but I shall nevertheless attempt to keep havoc at bay; I am determined, you see, that you should judge for yourself, rationally and impartially, the full extent of Fledge's duplicity. For it was at around this time—I can't be sure precisely when, sometime in October or November—that he set in motion the next stage of his plan, which involved the seduction of Harriet. And knowing what you do about the nature of Fledge's physical affections, you will recognize in this development just how far he was prepared to go to fulfill his ambition: he was prepared to assume the appetites of a normal man. Fledge's "normality" must be seen, then, for what it is: a sort of double inversion, an inversion of inversion itself.

But at the time I wasn't aware of any of this. At the time I had only the knowledge of what I'd seen in the pantry that night in September, and my suspicions regarding Sidney's disappearance. And what I'd seen in the pantry was not merely immoral, it was also criminal—men were once *hanged* for buggery, and not so long ago, either! Exposure meant publicity, it meant notoriety, complete loss of face and reputation, for the press, particularly the gutter press, tends to be shrill and vigorous in its condemnation of such offenses. Conscious as I was, then, of these factors, the farthest thing from my mind was the possibility of Fledge having designs on Harriet. It is only by going backwards, step-by-step, that I am able to reconstruct the probable course of the affair.

I hadn't sacked him as I'd intended to, you see. My interview with Sykes-Herring had gone well, surprisingly, and we had fixed a new date for the lecture, February 7, and shaken hands on it. This was what I'd gone to London for—I knew they didn't want me to speak, they were far too suspicious of my opinions, but if I could get a date and a handshake, then the gentlemanly code would ensure that on that day I would indeed have my podium and my audience. The point is, with the opportunity to get some real work done, I was loath to deal with the sort of distress that sacking the Fledges would provoke in Harriet. Cheap domestic servants were so hard to find, as she frequently reminded me, that losing these "treasures" would upset her for weeks. I decided to wait until I'd given my talk to the Royal Society; then they'd be out on their ears.

Harriet, I might add, was prepared to keep them on even after she'd learned Doris's "secret." "Hugo," she said to me one morning in a low voice, "I believe Mrs. Fledge drinks!"

"Of course she drinks, Harriet," I said, "anyone can see that from her nose." Harriet, in many ways, is an innocent.

"Do you suppose we should sack her?" she said. "Oh good Lord, we can't, Hugo! We were really so very lucky to get them, we'll never replace them at these wages. Do you realize what Connie Babblehump had to pay her last butler? And he wouldn't polish shoes!"

We were at breakfast. "Oh do be quiet, Harriet," I said from behind the *Times*. "Sack them if you want to, it's all the same to me." (I knew of course that she wouldn't.) "You hired them. Just don't gabble so."

"Hugo," she said, in a certain hurt tone that I knew well and enjoyed provoking, "you can be most horridly rude when you choose. Why do you choose?"

I said nothing to this; wasn't I the "impossible" man?

Soon enough the newspapers learned of Sidney's disappearance, and apparently decided that the situation was one that merited exploitation. The publicity was extremely unwelcome. After several very tiresome intrusions I instructed Fledge to turn away any reporters who came to the door, and George to see off trespassers, with a shotgun blast if necessary. The press, I should tell you, is no respecter of one's personal privacy. And in spite of everything they still clustered at the gates of Crook, and when Harriet tried to cycle into the village one morning she was literally mobbed, and had to dismount, and returned to the house in great distress. I was much relieved when, after a few days of rabid excitement, they lost interest in us, having fresh rubbish with which to titillate their readers. And mass literacy, they tell me, is a boon.

The days passed. The swallows flew away, the trees shed their leaves, and the garden grew less and less productive. It was damp and misty; it often rained. Cleo left for Oxford later in the month; she had been accepted at St. Anne's, to read moral philosophy. She only lasted a term, poor child. Sidney's disappearance upset her badly, she worried and worried at it, unable somehow to mesh the fact that he'd simply dropped out of sight into any workable picture of reality. She became convinced that evil had occurred, and nothing I could say would dissuade her of it. She tormented herself with the idea that someone, or something, had killed her Sidney—her sweet, gentle, spineless Sidney. Her ferret. Who could do such a thing? And why? It was not a happy Cleo who left us to begin her university life that October. I hold the newspapers responsible for putting those lurid and terrible ideas in her head. The irony was that I couldn't tell her that I knew Sidney was alive and well, lying low somewhere to avoid being blackmailed by Fledge. Then the whole story would have had to come out, and it was from precisely this that I was trying to shield the girl.

I did not dream of Doris again, I'm happy to say, after that extraordinary recrudescence of libido she aroused in me the night of the storm. I theorized that what had happened was that the frustration I'd been feeling with regard to the deferred lecture had by some odd psychic process been displaced, shunted sideways, as it were, into the realm of physical desire—a nice confusion, perhaps, of Logos and Eros. At any rate, as my work went forward in the autumn and early winter, I actually felt grateful for the delay. I was able to refine the thing, polish it, give it some style.

We had the first snow of the year on December 15. I awoke early, and through lead-latticed windows marbled with frost I glimpsed the dazzling whiteness of the countryside. I threw wide the windows, then, and stood, in my dressing gown, and smoking a cigar, as the sun began its low arc across the sky, picking diamonds of light from the snow as it went. My bedroom faces north, across the valley of the Fling to the wooded hills beyond, and in fields and lanes the tracks of birds and foxes were visible as faint wandering lines, slender as hairs, inscribed upon the natural world by its creatures. I imagined then the children of Ceck, their eyes ablaze with the primitive wonder of savages, and their noses squashed bloodless on chilled cottage windows, desperate to be out and trampling in the stuff, hurling it about, building men with it. This predilection we have for constructing effigies of ourselves—it is surely instinctual, witness the spontaneous behavior of children in snow.

Fledge appeared with my morning tea. "Snow at last, Fledge," I said, still gazing out across the fields.

"So it would appear, Sir Hugo," he said. "Will there by anything else, Sir Hugo?"

"No thank you, Fledge." He left the room. Only then did I turn from the window and approach my tea. So it would appear, Sir Hugo! That snow didn't "appear"; it existed! It was real! One could see it, touch it, taste it, probably smell it, if you had a good nose (I don't). Probably *hear* it, if you were an Eskimo! Fledge was a man who took not even the evidence of his senses on trust, and veiled his cynicism in that mannered cant he spoke. Christ how I hated him, him and his phlegmatic evasions, his low cunning, his secret lusts!

That evening, the evening of the first snow, Harriet and I sat as usual at the dinner table. Our talk was desultory. A dozen flames flickered on a branch of silver candlesticks as Fledge moved soundlessly around the table, removing a plate, refilling a glass (usually mine), generally performing his tasks with a scrupulous punctilio. A fire crackled in the hearth and once, high above, a wedge of snow slithered down the roof and landed with a soft thump on the path below. Otherwise Crook was still and silent, and slightly fragrant with the smell of the Christmas tree out in the hall. From the outside, to one coming up the drive, it must have seemed, with its snow-crusted gables, the holly wreath nailed over the porch, and the firelight gleaming through the mullioned windows, to emanate an aura of solidity and repose, of benevolence, warmth, and shelter. Ha! There was a snake in this garden, a worm in this bud! We were about to rise from the table when children's voices reached us. "Listen Hugo," whispered Harriet, and together we sat there, in the candlelight, straining to hear. "It's the carol singers."

We went to the front door, and opened it, and there, standing in a group, and flanked by two schoolteachers, each with a lantern mounted on a stick, were the children of Ceck Primary, all booted and hatted and warmly coated. Their reedy little voices rose over the gables of Crook, and from the kitchen Mrs. Fledge appeared, and came down the hall to listen. And then Fledge himself joined us, and to the strains of "Silent Night" we stood, together, in silence, though Doris was unable to stifle a sob (drunk no doubt).

When they had finished, in they all came, and the children went tramping down to the kitchen, where Doris gave them mince pies and lemonade. Harriet and I steered the teachers into the drawing room and made them drink whisky by the fire.

All of which, while no doubt arousing tender feelings in the hearts of the mawkish, promised nothing but disruption and distraction as far as I was concerned. I know the Christmas season for what it is, you see—a period of tedious social obligations, frenzied domestic activity, and unlimited opportunity for alcoholic excess. For one such as I, with an important lecture to prepare, it spelled disaster. Are you familiar, by the way, with the etymology of *mawkish*? It comes from an Old Norse word for maggot, or flesh worm, and means "nauseatingly insipid."

HARRIET IS A sentimental woman, and, as I say, an innocent. In many ways she is still the girl I married in 1921, and Fledge I imagine must have smiled inwardly at the ease with which he accomplished her seduction. Harriet had not led a happy life, she had not been fulfilled by the mature love of a devoted husband, for, as I think must be clear by now, I had been far too interested in my bones ever to give her the tenderness and candor that every woman needs from a man. There was, thus—and these insights, ironically enough, I have had the leisure to develop only since becoming paralyzed—a sort of aching void within her, a void she had for years attempted to fill with religion. This was why her priest, Pin, was so important to her—he was a surrogate of Jesus Christ, who was in turn a surrogate of *me*—the husband who had so utterly failed her.

Not that our marriage had been empty from the start, far from it. In the early days we shared a bedroom in the west wing and we were happy. The African expedition was still in the early planning stages, and I seemed, somehow, to have room in my life for both paleontology and love. Harriet was a sweet, vivacious girl, an English rose, people used to call her, on account of her complexion; and, seeing her with the clever, ambitious young naturalist I then was, they remarked on what a well-suited couple we seemed. What went wrong? I'd always assumed that our marriage began to founder only after I'd come back from Africa with George—that *Phlegmosaurus* had demanded so much of me, I'd allowed our love to die. But in fact— and this is another of those insights that came to me as I moldered in the alcove under the stairs—Harriet and I had stopped sleeping together even before I left for Africa.

One incident came back to me then with particular clarity. I remember the day—this must have been, oh, 1924, 1925—that Dome put up a picture on a wall of our bedroom, a framed reproduction of a watercolor called *The Virgin of the Lilies*. There was already a large wooden crucifix hanging over the bed, and the experience of going to sleep immediately beneath those bleeding feet I used to find distinctly macabre; but as I say, I loved Harriet then, and I tolerated it for her. But *The Virgin of the Lilies* was too much. The thing oozed a sort of sickly religiosity that frankly embarrassed me, and the idea that I would now have to spend my nights not only with Jesus Christ but with his mother as well was not to be borne. Down the stairs I clattered and had it out with Harriet there and then. Oh, there were tears, but I stood firm, young prig that I was in those days. Dome removed *The Virgin in the Lilies* that very afternoon, but somehow, after that, things were never the same between us. Actually, I believe she told Patrick Pin about it (that bloody priest has been in Ceck forever), and he began to turn her against me. By the winter of 1949 I had been sleeping over in the east wing for twenty-five years, and love—the love of a husband and a wife—had long since died between us. I can't say I missed it. I had my bones, as I say, and if I was *very* occasionally troubled with "urges" I would just slip down to the Hodge and Purlet, where a few hours in the company of men like John Crowthorne and George Lecky would get them out of my system. (This is why that dream about Doris Fledge was so disconcertingly bizarre.) But in all those years, it had never once occurred to me to wonder if Harriet was ever similarly afflicted, and if so, how she dealt with it. Hardly a thing one can discuss with a woman, after all.

But by ignoring Harriet all those years, I now realized, I had played right into Fledge's hands. For he awakened her, in a romantic sense, my sleeping beauty (ha!) and, brushing aside the religious sentiments with which she had for so long masked from herself her loneliness and frustration, he quickly dominated her heart, as a means of dominating my house.

Solitude is a terrible thing, for it permits the imagination to picture, in detail, that which perhaps should never be articulated. I saw it beginning in the larder, for some reason, that's where I saw Fledge making his first move, emerging from the underbrush of servility, as it were, to strike at the master. I imagine they were conducting one of Harriet's "inventories"; she does this every so often to ensure that we don't run out of food and starve to death.

The larder of Crook is a narrow room, high-ceilinged, dimly lit, its marble-tiled shelves crowded with jars of pickles and preserves, dried fruit and stewed fruit, leftovers of cold joints and milk puddings and jellies. Harriet—this is all conjectural, you must remember, but it hardly strains credibility, given what we already know—Harriet edges slowly forward between the shelves, her worried eyes scanning from side to side till she fetches up before the jams. She begins to count jars. Her hair, today, is pinned in a particularly lustrous and unruly bun; she turns to Fledge and asks him does he think we should order more from the village?

Fledge thinks not. A tall man, he peers at the high shelves and reads off the labels: "Plum jam, raspberry jam, strawberry jam, gooseberry jam. At least half-a-dozen of each, madam."

"*Is* there, Fledge?" says Harriet. "I had no idea we'd eaten so little jam."

Fledge turns to her in that narrow place. He cannot fail to notice how Harriet's eyes shine in the gloom, nor how a strand or two of her rich, coppery bun drifts loose of its pin and makes her look rather attractively distrait. And Harriet? What does she see, what does she feel? A vague tenderness for the man, possibly, such as she feels for most of humanity; she has never consciously examined her feelings, really; he is Fledge, he is the butler. But now she looks up into his face, and there between the pickled gherkins and the rhubarb chutney a rather warm, liquid event occurs inside her.

Suddenly, all is very still. The smile dies on Harriet's lips, but she does not look away: she has recognized the expression on Fledge's face. The silence throbs vibrantly in that ill-lit larder, and then he gently places a hand on the small of her back, and, with the other round her shoulders, he draws her to him and kisses her on the mouth.

Harriet closes her eyes. His kiss is firm, soft, hungry, sweet, and terribly, terribly arousing. Suddenly, oh how she wants him, his long pale slender body, his quiet, strong maleness—"Oh Fledge," she breathes. Her respiration is disturbed and the color has risen in her cheeks. She withdraws a little. She gazes at him with intense seriousness and then, lifting her arms, she links her fingers behind his neck and draws his face to hers once more. When they break apart this time tears are streaming down her cheeks and her mind is in turmoil. "Oh Fledge," she murmurs, "just hold me for a moment. I think I shall faint."

Fledge holds her, and Harriet slowly brings her breathing under control. She pulls a small handkerchief from the sleeve of her cardigan and dabs at her eyes, which shine now more radiantly than ever. "Oh Fledge," she says, with a small gurgle of laughter, then sniffs several times and blows her nose. Tucking the handkerchief back up her sleeve, she takes the butler's hands firmly in her own. "You are a dear man," she says, "but we must get on. Have we, dear Fledge, enough jam?"

"Yes madam," says Fledge. "We have enough jam."

FAITHLESS WOMAN! JEZEBEL! Oh

how I raged and seethed in my grotto, as my drooling
body snorted in that loud, piggy manner that had Doris
running down the hall to clap me on the back in case I
suffocated on my own phlegm! In time I calmed down,
and, when I could think again, it occurred to me that
if Harriet did, indeed, permit herself to surrender to
passion for a few brief moments in the larder, I should
not assume that a lifetime of devout Catholic practice
would thereupon simply collapse, regardless of the psy-
chology behind it, that a single kiss would usher in a
period of uncontrolled promiscuity. No, that would take
a little longer to come about. First there would have to
be the soul-searching.

I see Harriet in her bedroom in the west wing. She
has retired to write letters before lunch. But though her

fountain pen is filled, and the crested sheet of white bond lies before her on the leaf of her *escritoire*, no mark has yet appeared upon the virgin page. She gazes out of the window to the hills north of Crook, and watches a bird rising and falling on the currents of the clear, cold air, so distant as to seem no more than a speck. Her long-dormant sexuality has been awakened—is she to lay it to rest once more, let it sleep and be forgotten, as it has this last quarter-century, and *die*?

"Darling Hilary," she writes. "We are so looking forward to seeing you all for Christmas. Fledge and I were in the larder this morning, making sure there was enough jam in the house." Harriet stops writing and again gazes out of the window. This will not do, not at all. She screws up the sheet of notepaper and tosses it into her wastebasket. Fetching out a clean sheet, she writes: "Dear Fledge," and then sits once more with her eyes fixed on that far, circling bird and her pen poised, unmoving, at a shallow angle over the paper. Finally she rises to her feet and rings for him.

"Fledge," she says, turning to him as he silently materializes in the doorway of her bedroom. He is as inscrutable as ever, despite what has happened in the larder. His collar is spotless, his tailcoat perfectly pressed, the crease in his gray striped trousers as sharp as a blade. His oxfords shine with a dull gleam, as does his red-brown hair. His chin is impeccably shaved. "Madam?"

"Fledge, whatever were we thinking of this morning? We must have been mad! What if someone had seen us? Fledge, it must never be spoken of, and naturally it must never, ever happen again."

"Yes madam."

"That will be all."

Fledge bows, and retires.

One further incident is probably necessary before we send Harriet scurrying to her priest. I imagine it occurring a day or two later. Harriet is again in her room, and has just rung for her afternoon tea. She sits gazing at the picture I have already alluded to, *The Virgin of the Lilies*. Fledge knocks, and enters with her tea tray, and sets it down. Then, sinking to one knee beside her chair, he takes Harriet's hand and presses the palm to his lips.

"Oh Fledge," she murmurs, as the tears come. They come so easily, these days, for some reason. She reaches for him, opening her arms, and gathers him to her breast. She clings chastely to him for a few moments, weeping, and then becomes aware of his hand under her skirt upon the flesh of her inside thigh. "No!" she cries, thrusting him away. "No, Fledge, this is all wrong, all wrong!" She rises to her feet and moves away, nervously touching her hair, very flustered indeed. "Fledge, you must not do this. It's simply absurd of you to do this! Too absurd for words!"

Fledge has moved to the door; then he is gone, without a word, and the door closes with a soft click of the latch behind him. Harriet sinks into her chair once more and absently smooths her skirt where the man's hand crept under it. She gazes out unseeing over the bleak wintry countryside, and then her damp eyes return to the painting. From the foreground clusters of lilies tinted a delicate shade of mauve sweep back in a graceful curve to the figure of the Virgin, who clasps to her white-robed body the infant Jesus. She stands upon a bank of cloud, while far beneath a river winds through green and rolling countryside—countryside not unlike our own part of Berkshire, oddly enough. Harriet has often sat before this painting, pondering the ancient metaphorical association of altitude and divinity, and thinking of her dead savior. It is not Jesus Christ who occupies her thoughts now, however, but Fledge; and he is very much alive.

But perhaps you think I'm making all this up, perhaps you think these the delusions of a diseased imagination. Explain to me why, then, if Fledge had not seduced Harriet, and thus bent her to his will, she made no protest when he turned my wheelchair to the wall?

I WAS IN the barn on Christmas morning, the place rendered temperate by a pair of powerful hot-air blowers, when Fledge tapped at the door: Inspector Limp was waiting in the drawing room to see me. Now Crook tends to be rather crowded at Christmas, and most of the problem is the Horns. The Horns are the family of my elder daughter, Hilary, whom I may have mentioned to you. She takes after Harriet and has been terrified of me since early childhood. Every year she and her husband, Henry, an orthopedic surgeon who wears a thick black beard that makes him look like a sea captain (I used to tell people he earned his living making ships in bottles) bring their son, my grandson, Victor, now aged ten, down to Crook for Christmas. Harriet of course loves having them, and works herself into a fine dither as she fusses in advance over food, drink, the tree, the decorations, etc. Henry Horn is, I suppose, a tolerable enough fellow; he always takes a lively interest in my bones, and I in his, but quite frankly the only member of that family for whom I have any real affection is Victor.

Victor Horn is a true Coal. He is a fat boy with a thick fringe of brown hair that falls into his eyes rather as Cleo's does. He has Cleo's teeth, too, *Coal* teeth, and when he grins, which is often, his cheeks plump up to shiny freckled balls and his front teeth protrude far and goonishly over his lower lip. A precocious child, he had brought a volume of Freud with him, *Totem and Taboo*, never read it myself, and told me very seriously that he planned to become a psychoanalyst. The point is, that when all these people are about it is much harder than usual for me to maintain an atmosphere of slightly sulky gloom in the house; there's altogether far too much jollity. Actually, it wasn't quite so bad this year, for Cleo's depression cast something of a general pall over the proceedings.

They were all at Mass in the village when Limp came to call. A small bald man in a long gray raincoat, he apologized for disturbing my Christmas and asked me to go down to the station with him. I agreed, of course. We drove into Ceck and I was led through the tiny police station and into the back room, which was bare but for a simple wooden table, two upright chairs, and, leaning against the wall, something cloaked in a heavy, dark green tarpaulin. The Ceck policeman stood beside it. "All right Cleggie," said Limp, and the policeman removed the tarpaulin.

It was a bicycle, a high, black one. Splinters of ice

and frozen clods of mud clung to it; small dirty puddles were already forming on the floor as they melted and fell off. A number of spokes on the back wheel were bent, and the saddle had been twisted around backwards. Limp asked me if I'd ever seen it before. "Yes," I said. I knew that bicycle. I used to ride it myself. It had been dug up in the Ceck Marsh that morning, after a handlebar was reported poking up through a fissure in the frozen earth. "Is that," said Limp, "the bicycle Sidney Giblet was riding the night he disappeared?"

"Yes," I said, "it is."

I returned to Crook. A large number of Roman Catholics were milling about the drawing room, drinking my sherry and eating ham sandwiches. "There you are, dear," said Harriet, coming forward to peck my cheek. "Fledge told us Inspector Limp came for you. We thought you'd been thrown in clink."

"Nothing of the sort," I replied. I groped about for some suitable fiction. "Just some silly nonsense about poachers."

"Poachers!" cried Connie Babblehump. I groaned inwardly. "Curse of the countryside," she declared.

"Mantraps," said Freddy Hough, a magistrate. "That's the answer. Big pair of iron jaws, with a spring. Chap steps on it—*snap*!"

"Freddy, really," said Harriet quietly.

"Take his leg right off," said Freddy, then swallowed the remains of his sandwich and washed it down with a mouthful of amontillado. "That old rogue Crowthorne," he said, "he's the worst."

I was quiet and subdued the rest of the day. Nobody

noticed, I think, what with the presents being opened and the flurry of preparations for dinner. Patrick Pin traditionally ate his Christmas dinner at Crook, so after Harriet's guests had gone I permitted myself to be drawn into light eschatological chat by the drawing-room fire. I have no great liking for Patrick Pin; I believe he tries to turn people against me because I refuse to accept transubstantiation. But this particular afternoon I was preoccupied with what I'd seen at the police station, and remained civil. The smells drifting down the passage from the kitchen grew increasingly tantalizing as the afternoon drew on. We ate at six; Victor was very jolly, having been allowed a glass of beer.

When it was all over, and the turkey and the ham had been largely demolished, a soporific reaction set in, a digestive torpor, and I decided to go down to Ceck's Bottom and mull things over for a while. This was actually something I did every year, a facet of my role as landlord and squire.

George was standing, grinning, at the head of the table, wielding a long, sharp, bone-handled carving knife in one hand, a fork in the other, and cutting steaming slices of meat from a large haunch of pork. Frank Bracknell was there, and Bill Cudlip (sexton and gravedigger), and old John Crowthorne of course. All were in braces and shirtsleeves, for the stove was stoked and burning, and all were drinking beer from large, froth-ringed glasses. Someone, from an impulse probably pagan in origin, had nailed sprigs of holly and mistletoe to various jambs and lintels, and several wooden crates of brown ale were stacked by the back door. As the room steamed up the men received heaped plates of roast meat and potatoes from George; they sat there like feasting gods, like woodland deities, these satyrs of Ceck, and their talk was brusque and clipped and jocular. The candles flickered, the lamps glowed, and I could feel the spirits of deep winter drifting over the cold, snow-covered, moon-silvered country outside. I sank into a chair in the corner, accepted a glass of beer, and pondered the implications of the morning's revelation. I could make no sense of it. Why would the boy bury his bicycle? I allowed my mind to go blank, my thoughts to wander, and slowly, in my imagination, a picture began to form.

It was night. I saw a man on a bicycle, with a load on his shoulder, pedaling toward me down the Ceck's Bottom road. It was a bulky load, all tied up in an old sack, and it flopped about as the bicycle glided through the shadows of oak boughs and foliage. He sat up very erect in the saddle, this dark rider, and as he drew close I recognized something familiar in the stiffness of his figure. It was not until he passed through a pool of blotchy moonlight, however, that I was able to make out his features. It was Fledge, of course; and as he turned off down the cart track I realized with a lurch of shock that what he carried in the sack on his shoulder could only be the body of Sidney Giblet: *he was taking it out to the marsh*.

What did this mean? What was I trying to tell myself? Why would he be carting Sidney's body out to the marsh? Then slowly, and with a dawning sensation of horror, I realized that I'd got the whole thing the wrong way round, completely arse-backwards. It was

Fledge who was being blackmailed by *Sidney*, I realized, not vice versa, and for this he had murdered the boy. I sat up rigid in my chair, the beer glass suspended halfway to my lips. But why, I thought? What was at stake, that he would murder for it? What on earth would justify murder? And it was then, for the first time, that I glimpsed the true outline of the fiend's design: He had murdered Sidney to prevent the boy from disturbing his scheme to usurp *me*—the bastard was after my house!

I drained off my beer and returned in my mind to the marsh; and now I saw him standing on the edge of a pit he had dug, at the bottom of which lay a blackly gleaming pool of water. I saw him guide the bicycle over the edge, and I saw it tip, and fall, and splash to rest in the black water at the bottom. He stood there at the edge of the pit, framed against the moon, and it was as though *I* were at the bottom, gazing up at him. But why didn't he toss the sack in too? Why hadn't the sack come up with the bicycle? This was strange. I frowned. I lit a cigar. I sank back into the chair, and allowed my mind to drift once more. And it occurred to me then that perhaps he had been disturbed in his work, that he had heard someone coming through the trees, and been forced to creep off into the darkness—to come back later and fill in the pit. But if he'd been surprised in this way (so ran my reasoning), it was unlikely he'd have been able to haul off the bulk of a sacked corpse with him, it was far too cumbersome; and if this was so, if he'd crept off without it—and for some weird reason I felt certain that this indeed was what had happened— then whoever it was had disturbed him would have come upon the ghastly thing, and then, improbable though it may seem, would have *removed it* from the vicinity of the bicycle pit. Again I sat up in my chair, puffing energetically on my cigar. Was this feasible? It did at least explain why the bicycle had come up but not the sack. But if it furnished an answer to that question, it raised the even more perplexing one of *why the other man had failed to report what he'd found*.

And it was at *that* point I realized I could think of only four men who would be out on the Ceck Marsh at that time of night; and all four were at that very moment sitting with me in George Lecky's kitchen, barking with laughter as they swallowed brown ale.

I DID NOT get any further with my speculations that night. Frankly, I backed off; these were men I'd known for many years, all my life in the case of Crowthorne, Cudlip, and Bracknell, and it was impossible to imagine any of them trying to dispose of a corpse in some improper manner. I decided to suspend my hypothesis for the time being, and await new facts. This is the inductive method; it had guided my thinking for over thirty years.

What I dreaded now, having made a positive identification of the bicycle, was breaking the news to Cleo. At first she took it like a Coal, square on the chin. "I knew it," she muttered, clenching her fists and taking a number of deep breaths. It was Boxing Day, we were in my study, and Harriet, whom I'd already told, was sitting anxiously on the edge of an armchair, ready with the solace of the maternal bosom. But the maternal bosom, it seemed, was not needed. Pressing her lips together and frowning darkly, the girl turned toward the fire and, plunging her hands into the pockets of her skirt, gazed for a few moments into the flames. "Well," she said, looking up at last, brisk and brave, "it rather looks as if Sidney came to grief on the marsh after all. You see, I've been expecting this; I *knew*."

Harriet, who had half risen from her chair, anticipating a flood of tears—and ready to tell Cleo that the bicycle being found proved nothing at all—sank back, and a rather puzzled concern clouded her features. "Darling," she said, "what do you mean, you *knew*?"

A most peculiar thing happened then. There was a sudden flare of energy in Cleo, but it was a strange, wild energy. She *laughed*, you see, in a joyless, manic sort of way, and cried out, "What I say, Mummy! I *knew*! He came and told me!"

"Darling, do sit down, please. *Who* told you?"

"*He* did! Sidney did!" And then she burst into tears and flung herself into an armchair, where she buried her face in her hands and sobbed convulsively. Harriet was beside her instantly. "But darling, darling—"

With an awful wail Cleo brushed her mother aside and fled from the room. Harriet gazed at me, dumb with shock, and then went after the girl. "No, Harriet," I said sharply, "let her go." Harriet paused, her hand on the doorknob; she turned toward me. "Let her go," I said quietly, and crossing the room, I led her back to her armchair by the fire, where she sat in a state of dazed dismay while I made her a drink.

I SIT HERE in my cave, in my *grotto*, and think of Cleo, Cleo with her buckteeth and lively eyes, her elfin presence, her quick, light ways . . . Did I mention that the only good that has come of this term I've spent among the ontologically dead has been Cleo's sympathy? That sympathy has, alas, become rarer and more fleeting; the scene I have just described, in which she told us that she knew what had happened to Sidney, that he had told her, was the first indication to Harriet and myself that something was seriously amiss with our daughter; it was, in fact, the first manifestation of a mental illness that has, in recent months, progressively enshrouded her mind. She does have moments of lucidity—inspired lucidity—and it was during one of these that she saw what all the rest of them are blind to, that

I, Hugo, am still thinking and feeling within the frame of this inert and failing flesh.

You see, after my cerebral accident Crook entered a period of tranquillity. The storm of my personality had ceased to rage, and a smooth calm settled on the surface of life, a deceptive calm, I believe, that concealed within it the workings of dark and restless forces—but a calm, nonetheless. I was much alone, in those early days after leaving the hospital, with the grotesques of my imagination; and when I believed myself unobserved, I would at times permit myself to weep, as I contemplated my own ruin and the ruin of my house. The day I sat facing the wall and, hearing the sounds of a chess game behind me, imagined a scene of venereal depravity—that day I permitted the tears to fall, and when Cleo entered the drawing room and with a cry of indignation turned my wheelchair to the light, she saw the tears and, suddenly quiet, sank to her knees beside me, and bringing her face close to mine, gazed into my eyes—and *saw me*. "Daddy," she breathed, her face still but a few inches from mine, so that I gazed back at eyes the precise same shade of gray as my own, "Daddy," she whispered, "you're in there, I know you are." And from that moment forward I was no longer alone. Fledge knew, of course, but he used the knowledge to torment me. Cleo loved me.

But as I say, Cleo is rarely with us anymore. Like me she has been trapped in a false world of shadows and phantoms; for her, as for me, the borders and boundaries of the real and the fantastic have become blurred, unreliable, faulty. In her, as in me, order is crumbling. But I at least can see it crumbling. Cleo cannot do even that, or rather, she does it increasingly rarely. In fact, in these last days her recognition of my own sentient existence has grown so sporadic that she no longer provides me any real support. It is Fledge, ironically, who maintains me—he maintains me with his hatred. I think that were he to cease to hate me, were he to deprive me of this last fragile link, this last *relation* with the world, then I should be swallowed up, sink into darkness for good. Doubtless there would be a final gasp, a last solipsistic flurry of ideation, but then I would fall silent, truly become the vegetable the world takes me for. This, as I say, is the irony of my existence, that I have come to require the hatred of a bad servant simply to *be*. Ontologically I am not dead, but I am clinging to the ledge with my fingernails!

But Cleo. It was of Cleo, not myself, that I intended to speak, for as I say, with her mysterious declaration that Sidney had told her what had happened to him, Harriet and I first began to understand how deeply the loss of the boy had touched her. "Let her go, Harriet," I had said in the study that night; I knew that, like me, Cleo would prefer to recover from an access of intense emotion privately and alone, that she would seek us out as and when she wished to speak about it, and not before. For the next two days, then, a pall of sadness lay upon the house, as the fact of Cleo's grief permeated the atmosphere. Everybody felt it, everybody understood it. The girl came down to meals but was silent and listless. Her face, normally so lively, so mobile, rapidly and dramatically reflected her inner state—dark shadows appeared around her eyes, her cheeks seemed to hollow out, to become gaunt and harrowed with pain.

We all felt for her, and waited for her to begin to come to terms with her emotions. That process was disturbed, however, by two events; and the first of these was the pipes of Crook bursting.

It was my grandfather, a farsighted and energetic Victorian called Sir Digby Coal, who introduced indoor plumbing to Crook. The household is today still served by the lavatories he installed, which, in their day, were much admired: the seats and covers were of pale oak, all the brass fittings shone like gold, and the bowls were sculpted from the finest white china. The tank is in the attic, and Sir Digby did not rest until the flushing mechanism functioned to that standard of efficiency that his generation brought to bear on everything it undertook. For Sir Digby Coal, even the humble lavatory served to express the idea of Progress.

But last winter Crook experienced a cold snap that was suddenly, in the days after Christmas, punctuated by a thaw, and Sir Digby's obsolescent and cantankerous pipes promptly burst. A crisis ensued: the kitchen was flooded, and the central heating, senile and inefficient though it was, had to be shut down. There was no running water. In the very somber atmosphere that had descended upon us, it was as though the house were performing its own tearful requiem for Sidney Giblet, a sort of gesture of hydraulic condolence. So it was that on New Year's Eve we all sat down to a breakfast of deviled kidneys amid the noise and clatter of the Ceck plumber and his two sons; and where before had reigned the hushed silence appropriate to the situation, there was now the sloshing of mops, the banging of spanners, and the cheery, whistling bustle of men at work. And as we sat in this din, the telephone suddenly raised its shrill mechanic voice. Some moments later Fledge materialized at my elbow.

"Telephone, Sir Hugo."

Down the table eyes were lifted in mild curiosity, except Victor's; he was deep in his Freud.

"Who is it, Fledge?"

Hilary began to smear marmalade on a piece of toast. Harriet was stirring her tea. I folded the *Times*.

"It's Mrs. Giblet."

"Oh *no*!" This from Cleo, who rose from the table and left the room.

I returned to the dining room five minutes later. An expectant hush greeted my reentry. "Well?" said Harriet. I sat down. I told Fledge to give me more tea. I then reported that Mrs. Giblet had been informed by Inspector Limp about the bicycle being dug up in the marsh. That, I said, was not all. Considering herself qualified to furnish some real assistance to the police (of whose intelligence she was apparently no great admirer), she had traveled to Ceck, and was even now ensconced in the Hodge and Purlet.

A gasp from Harriet. "Oh good heavens," she said, gazing at me with genuine distress. "Hugo, must we have her here? We must."

"I explained to Mrs. Giblet about our pipes," I replied. "I told her she would be more comfortable where she was."

"Well that's a relief, at any rate," murmured Harriet.

"I did, however, feel obliged to ask her to dine with us tonight."

"Yes, of course," said Harriet. "Oh dear, poor woman. She's probably just as upset as Cleo. More so!" She sighed. She had already extended her full sympathy, as a woman and as a mother, to that ghastly old battle-ax, that dragon, who had settled now in our midst and would undoubtedly belch flame and ill-smelling smoke into all our lives. I made for the barn, reflecting, not for the first time, that if I'd had the slightest inkling of the trouble Sidney Giblet was going to cause, I'd never have let him within a mile of Crook in the first place.

The last night of the old year; and seven of us sat down to dinner. Next to me and to my left was Mrs. Giblet. She had arrived at Crook in a vast and shapeless fur coat with padded shoulders, and a black hat whose brim was pinned up on one side and embellished with sprigs of lace and crimson cherries. In one arm she clutched her lapdog; with the other she gripped the handle of her rubber-tipped walking stick, the one with the skull embedded in the crook. She wore gloves of black satin and a large white pearl in each pendent and withered earlobe. Fledge attempted to take her coat from her, but she insisted on keeping it on for the time being, until she was "adjusted." Wily old bird, she realized immediately of course that in a house like this the central heating was probably tepid at the best of times. With burst pipes we had only fires to warm us, and Crook is a house of drafts.

Along the hallway she advanced, inspecting as she

went and nodding to left and right with royal approbation. Her entry into the drawing room was stately; Henry and Victor both rose to their feet, and Harriet came forward with both arms outstretched. "Dear Mrs. Giblet," she said warmly, "how good of you to come at such short notice."

It was the perfect thing to say to Mrs. Giblet. "Not at all, Lady Coal," she purred. "Ah! Cleo!" Cleo came forward quietly and brushed the old woman's cheek with her lips. Mrs. Giblet then sank into the armchair Henry had vacated by the fire, and began to fumble for cigarettes. Harriet introduced her to the Horns, apologized profusely for the cold, and invited her to have a glass of sherry. Mrs. Giblet thought that would be nice. Then, failing altogether to beat about the bush, she declared to the room at large: "I have met the man Limp. Sir Hugo"—she wheeled about in her chair—"I am surprised that you place any confidence in him at all; to my mind he is a total incompetent."

I frowned. "He has had very little to work with, Mrs. Giblet," I said.

"That's a moot point, Sir Hugo. With all the progress Limp is making we'll be lucky to see Sidney in a box. I'm sorry, my dear"—Cleo had been unable to suppress a small cry—"but there's no use holding out false hopes."

She puffed lugubriously at her cigarette. A silence fell. The light died in her eyes and her face slowly collapsed, and in the sag of it there seemed to dwell such an immense despair that the atmosphere rapidly became very black indeed. Harriet rushed in to fill the breach. "Mrs. Giblet," she cried, "come! There is no reason to despair, none at all. I keep telling Cleo, digging up a bicycle tells us nothing at all."

Mrs. Giblet looked up. She reached for Harriet's hand, and smiled that oddly charming smile I'd seen in London. "Of course it doesn't," she said. "Lady Coal, forgive me for infecting your home with my gloom. May I, I wonder, have more of that sherry? It really is very good." And while Fledge was busy with the task, Mrs. Giblet, apparently somewhat "adjusted," opened her coat. "Thank you," she said, raising her face to Fledge, as he appeared with her sherry. "Personally," she said, "I intend to go over the Ceck Marsh with a fine-tooth comb. You may be right about Limp, Sir Hugo, or then again you may not. I should simply like to convince myself that nothing has been overlooked. Would anyone, I wonder, care to help me?"

The brief silence that followed upon this bizarre invitation was broken by Victor. "Yes," he cried, with alacrity, "I would!" This functioned as a piece of comic relief, although the boy was quite serious. A ripple of amusement passed over the drawing room, and then Fledge announced that dinner was served.

Going in to dinner, Mrs. Giblet attached herself to Harriet, to whom she had apparently taken a "shine," and gushed. "All this *wood*, Lady Coal, how comforting it must be to live in a house with walls paneled with *wood*. Oak, I imagine, isn't it? Good English oak; it makes for a feeling of continuity with the past, is what I've always thought. Are you a great believer in tradition, Lady Coal?"

"I suppose I am, Mrs. Giblet," murmured Harriet.

Patrick McGrath

"I, too, am deeply conservative," said Mrs. Giblet. "I always have been. Churchill's my man; I knew him once, you know. Brilliant chap, erudite, extremely, and such wit!" The old lady chuckled slightly and tapped Harriet's arm, upon which rested her own gnarled old claw. "Why once—but no, you don't want to hear my stories, do you. Up here, next to Sir Hugo? Delighted. Thank you, Fledge."

Seven of us, as I say, sat down to dinner that night, and a curious-looking group we made. With the central heating shut down, Crook was really very chilly, and in view of this fact I had decided that jerseys might be worn with evening dress. We thus had the spectacle of Henry Horn in a thick gray fisherman's sweater that bulked clumsily under his dinner jacket and, in concert with his beard, made him look more than ever like a sea captain. Hilary, Harriet, and Cleo all looked very gauche, all in their thickest cardigans, with headscarves tied under their chins. Victor was hardy, and wore only his school uniform; and Mrs. Giblet, having, clearly, adjusted, and no doubt thinking it highly improper, regardless of climatic conditions, to dine in a country house in her coat, had slipped the great fur off her shoulders and was revealed in the full majesty and splendor of her evening gown.

It was a black satin garment that had resided, I hypothesized, for a good forty years in some mahogany wardrobe in that dingy house near the British Museum. It was shiny and sleeveless, and hung to the ground in stiff folds, and rustled, I noticed, when she moved. As she seated herself by me, I became aware of a distinct smell of mothballs; nor was that the only smell that

116

clung to the woman. Rather, it served as a sort of deep bass to a veritable symphony of aromas, the melody, so to speak, being carried by a sharp little perfume which, so she told me (for I inquired) had been purchased in Strasbourg in 1934. Its sour and astringent qualities were vulgarized, however (my own nose, though not good, detected this), by a liberal application of cheap eau-de-cologne, and the whole was grimly inflected with the mundane odors of cigarette smoke, sherry, and the perfectly natural emanations of an aging flesh.

Her shoulders were bare, as were her upper arms, from which the skin hung in copious limp pouches. She'd donned her jewelry for dinner in the country, a tiara dotted with a diamond or two, and a string of pearls that dipped alarmingly toward the chasm that gaped within her bosom. The satin gloves reached to her elbows; she had wondered, she confided to me, whether they might not be a trifle *dressy* outside London. I assured her that, on the contrary, one could never be overdressed in the country, temperatures did not permit it. She took this quip in good humor. She ate well, occasionally dropping morsels to the beast in her lap, and she was deeply appreciative of my claret, which she loudly swilled about her mouth and swallowed with evident pleasure. I found myself, surprisingly, warming rather to the old buzzard, the old *turkey*, and when, apropos a remark of mine about a piece of fossilized bone with which I was much preoccupied at the time, she began to speak about her arthritis, I told her in an undertone that the man near the other end of the table, the one she'd taken for a sea captain, was in fact one of the best orthopedic surgeons in the country, and that after dinner she should tell *him* about her arthritis. She said she would. Henry, I thought, will be delighted.

The soup came and went, and then the main course—Doris had outdone herself with a joint of roast beef, and there was ham as well—and we were on to the Stilton when Cleo could finally contain herself no longer. She had been very quiet all evening; and now, as Mrs. Giblet demurely accepted more port from Fledge, and raised her glass to Henry, whom she had clearly earmarked as her healer, Cleo rose to her feet, perceptibly quivering with emotion, and pointed an unsteady finger at the old woman. "How *can* you?" she cried, and a strange, unnaturally fierce light burned in her eyes. "How *can* you sit and stuff yourself when Sidney's still *out there* somewhere, in the cold, in pain? Oh, you disgust me—no Mummy, don't try and shut me up, this is true—you sit here as if nothing had happened, when all the time the most appalling things are happening"—her finger swung round to the window—"out there! Outside! You have no *conception* of the evil that exists out there! You think the worst thing in the world is a burst pipe or a gamy ham, and all the time, right under your noses, the most foul and loathsome evil thing creeps on the earth, and you don't see it, you make yourselves blind to it because it's just too much trouble! Oh, if it touched your comfort, that would be different, but just the fact that a hideous, stinking, *evil* thing is crawling around outside this house—*that* won't rouse you, but it's there all the same! It's there! And you'll find it, Mrs. Giblet, you'll find it, out in the marsh, but you better go after dark! Oh! Oh!"—and she burst into tears and fled weeping from the room.

* * *

There was a brief bewildered silence. Then Harriet rose and followed Cleo, and then Hilary. I did not try to stop them. Then Mrs. Giblet spoke. "Poor child," she said, with a sigh. "I will tell her that we all feel as she does. But young people do like to see feelings displayed; they can't understand that with the years one learns to preserve one's energies; one has to. Is that not so, Sir Hugo?"

I had listened to Cleo's outburst with my elbows on the table, my forearms forming an arch, and my mouth and chin pressed to the interlocked fingers at its cusp. I glanced sideways at the old woman, but, knowing what I knew, I did not shift my head from my hands to respond. Instead, Victor spoke. "Daddy," he said, "I think that's hysteria, but I'm not sure what sort."

"Victor," said his father, "shut up."

THE HORNS WENT back to London at the beginning of January. They had not had a terribly festive time of it at Crook, I'm afraid. Sidney's specter had hovered over all of us, particularly Cleo of course, and what with the pipes bursting, the atmosphere in the house had been not only cheerless but uncomfortably cold and drafty as well. Hilary told Harriet that she was reluctant to go, with Cleo so unhappy, but Victor had to be back at school. Harriet assured her that she could cope perfectly well here. It was all very distressing. Henry actually drew me aside, just before they were to leave, and told me he was quite concerned about Cleo. He thought he detected a morbid element in her grief; this disturbed him. He suggested that if she was still depressed in a week or so we should telephone him; he would arrange for her to "see someone" in Harley

Street. I told him I appreciated his concern. But I was sure, I said, there was no cause for alarm. Didn't he know, I said, that all the Coals were mad? He ought to know, having married one of them! I grinned at him around my cigar and clapped him on the back. I asked him where his next voyage would take him, what far-flung corner of the globe—Singapore? The Caribbean? Or maybe the pine-girt shores of British Columbia, for a cargo of good pulping timber!

"Seriously, Hugo," he said.

"Seriously, Henry," I said, "don't worry about Cleo; she'll be fine with us."

I was sorry to see Victor go, I was fond of that little chap. I gave him a ten-shilling note when his parents weren't looking and told him to forget Freud, read Darwin instead. "Read *The Origin of the Species*, my boy," I said. "Find out where you came from." His hair falling over his eyes in a thick fringe, he grinned at me in mock outrage, those good Coal teeth of his protruding far beyond the bottom lip, and ran a plump finger across his throat. "Never!" he said. I cuffed him once or twice, shook his hand, and stamped off to the barn.

Mrs. Giblet was as good as her word. She resumed her tenure at the Hodge and Purlet, and early in the new year I began to hear reports from the village about her. She would apparently leave the inn after breakfast and be driven down the Ceck's Bottom road far as the cart track that gives onto the marsh. She would then make her way out onto the marsh and spend the day, in her huge fur coat, picking slowly across the frozen ground until, at around five, when the light began to thicken, she returned to the road, where the car would pick her up. Several people saw her out there, including Bill Cudlip and old John Crowthorne, and they mentioned it to me with quiet expressions of scorn. I found it oddly touching, though, the picture of the old woman, out on the marsh alone beneath the cold gray sky, searching for traces of her lost son. I presumed she did not follow Cleo's advice and go out there after dark, when the "evil creeping thing" was abroad; the Ceck Marsh, after dark, is an uncanny sort of place, even without evil creeping things. I was out there one night myself.

As for Cleo, she went into semi-seclusion over in the east wing, where she has her bedroom, and only rarely came downstairs. When she did appear, she was either angry or depressed or both. "Where," I chided, "has my laughing girl gone?"

She rounded on me, eyes blazing. "Why should I laugh, Daddy? What do I have to laugh about?"

"Steady, darling," murmured Harriet. "Not so *fierce*, darling." Then the girl started to cry, and Harriet had to comfort her. Harriet later came to me, worried, and asked me didn't I think we should call Henry and have someone "see" Cleo, as he'd suggested? Nonsense, I said, she'll pull through. Perfectly normal thing, no cause for alarm. Coals don't go to shrinks, I said. Very well, said Harriet, but I could see she wasn't altogether convinced.

But what had been uppermost in my mind, ever since Sidney's bicycle came up on Christmas Day, was the Fledge question. I was now certain that he must have ambushed the boy on his way into Ceck that night, murdered him, and then abandoned the body out on the marsh. But where *was* the body? You see my predicament? Even though I was certain in my own mind what had happened, I was hardly in a position to go to the police. I needed *facts*, I needed *evidence*—I needed a body, above all! I would just have to wait a little longer, and keep in the forefront of consciousness the knowledge that I was harboring under my roof a desperate and violent man—a cold-blooded killer, in fact.

JANUARY WAS, ON the surface, a period of calm, and though I was maintaining a discreet surveillance of Fledge I spent most of my time out in the barn, where I was putting the finishing touches to the lecture. I've told you how conducive to clear thinking I found the Ceck Marsh, particularly when I was in the throes of composition. I drove out there one Saturday afternoon toward the end of the month and parked the Morris, as was my habit, on the cart track that gave off the Ceck's Bottom road.

The ground was muddy, for we had had some rain, and the sky was gray and overcast. I squelched down the track in my Wellington boots and then, emerging from the trees, I experienced something of a shock— for the wide expanse of marsh that I had expected to find desolate and empty was, instead, peopled—there were figures in the landscape, tiny figures spread out in a long line against the horizon. I had at first no inkling of what this could mean. I knew that the police had gone over the marsh in late December, after finding the bicycle, but they had uncovered nothing more and so discontinued their search. But I soon recognized a familiar humped and shuffling form that, distant and indistinct though it was, could only be Mrs. Giblet. And the little figures abreast of her, moving slowly through the gloom of the afternoon—these were surely children!

I did not go further. The marsh was no use to me unless I found solitude there. I returned to the car and as I started it up a gentle, drizzling rain began to fall. I backed out into the road and turned in the direction of Ceck's Bottom. The light was perceptibly fading when I reached the farm. I found George in his slaughterhouse, a dimly lit shed that reeked of offal beneath an old roof of corrugated tin on which the rain came softly pattering down. It was a dark and primal place, George's slaughterhouse, and old John Crowthorne was in there with him, the pair of them in long, filthy aprons caked with blood; they were butchering the carcass of a freshly killed pig. It was a huge animal, and it was hanging upside down from its trotters from a hook in the beam overhead, sliced down the belly. Two buckets of faintly steaming blood stood on the floor nearby. George saw me in the doorway. He promptly whacked his chopper into a block of scarred wood and, wiping his hands on his apron, followed me out into the damp murk of the yard. His eyebrows meshed in an angry frown when I told him what I'd seen on the marsh, but it caused him no surprise. It seemed that the old woman was employing the children of Ceck in her search for the remains of Sidney; she gave them each sixpence for a day's work. Apparently she had a theory that when the earth thawed it tended to shift about, and in its shifting about to disgorge its contents, unless they were deeply buried. There was some thawing that January; Mrs. Giblet hoped it would cause to rise that which had remained buried during the police search.

We had a smoke, and then George tramped back across his dung-running farmyard to the shed. The rain came drizzling down upon him, and a sudden gust of wind molded his shirt to the ridges and hollows of his long, knobbled back. He reached the door of the shed, turned, and through the scrim of rain I watched him lift a hand and bare his big teeth at me. I touched the horn of the Morris and pulled out onto the Ceck's Bottom road, just as it began to rain in earnest. I mention this meeting only to demonstrate that George gave me no inkling, none at all, that he did, in fact, know what had happened to Sidney's body. Hardly surprising that he gave no sign of it; he was a dour and cryptic man at the best of times, and certainly knew how to keep a thing to himself.

I presume it was because I'd been out to the marsh in the afternoon that I dreamed of a Mesozoic swamp that night. It was very early in the morning, in the dream, and a sort of bluish gloom suffused the scene. Through a low fog that clung to the surface of the swamp darted small, shadowy, flying creatures that jinked and glided on delicate leathery webbed wings as they swept back and forth in search of prey. The tropical forest fringing the swamp was already steaming in the damp heat of dawn, and but for the steady buzzing and grating and chirping of the insects in the stands of giant pine and redwood nearby, a thick, heavy silence lay upon the place. Vast fallen tree trunks, indistinct in the gloom, their jagged stumps clawing high in the air like great drowning fingers, and trailing clumps and sheets of moss, lay moldering on the edge of the swamp, sinking back into the primeval slime from which they had originally risen. From out of one of these huge dead trunks there suddenly darts a tiny mammalian creature, covered with hair. It stops, one paw raised and its little snout twitching, then thirstily drinks from a pool of brackish black water puddled in the mud. Up comes that timid, twitching, hairy little head once more, and then the animal slips quickly back into its tree, back to its lair. A moment later a sort of muted rumbling sound can be heard from the forest, the crashing of huge bodies advancing through the undergrowth.

The light is growing stronger. All is quiet as death, out there on the swamp, as from the forest the din of approaching huge beasts grows thunderous. And then they appear through the trees, plodding along in single file, their little heads nodding from side to side from long swaying necks and vast, barrel-shaped bodies: a herd of gentle *Brontosauri*, small-brained herbivores, a dozen of them, coming to the swamp to drink. Their gray, leathery hides are blotched and stippled with faint, rust-red markings, and their long, tapering tails are held out stiffly behind them, the whiplike tips flicking back and forth as they come. They move with dogged and stately grace toward a pool of water in the center of the swamp, and their footpads make great gloopy sucking noises in the mud. A low mist still clings in wisps and streaks to the surface of the swamp, lending the creatures a vaguely phantasmal aspect. But the sky is growing lighter by the moment, the great blocks of shadow framing the swamp are fading, and the trees come dimly into view. On they plod, beneath a sky in which the undersides of a few fleecy clouds are touched now with the rich pinks and reds of the dawn.

They reach the pool and stand at the edge to drink. Their long tails still flick from side to side, and at every moment a head comes up, tiny on its serpentine neck, to sniff the air. The first rays of the morning sun come shafting through the forest and, catching the great back of one of these monsters, brings out the richly mottled russet redness of its hide; and still the heads go up and down, up and down, as from the forest comes the shrill scream of some awakening creature, followed by a long-drawn-out burst of manic chatter. A flying lizard drifts over the trees then wheels sharply and flaps off toward the rising sun. It is then that three events occur in rapid succession. The first is the springing up of a brisk breeze, blowing from the south; from that direction then comes the sound of some big animal moving through the trees; and a moment later the largest of the brontosaurs, a massive bull dinosaur of at least thirty tons, sniffs the air with intense concentration, then utters a sort of distressed whinny.

All drinking ceases. The brontosaurs stand rigid, their heads lifted as they catch the first faint traces of putrid meat drifting on the breeze. There is some shuffling, and more whinnying, as they recognize the unmistakable fetor of a predatory carnosaur—such creatures invariably stink of the carcass of their last meal, for they lie upon the rotting corpse for weeks, in a deep digestive torpor. And then the predator shows himself at the edge of the swamp: a full-grown, mature adult male *Phlegmosaurus carbonensis*.

At the sight of him panic catches hold of the timid brontosaurs. The dawn is shattered by great trumpetings of terror as they flounder in the mud, desperate to get off the swamp and back into the shelter of the trees. But in their hysteria they seem only to mire themselves deeper in the ooze.

The mud churns and flies as the trumpeting brontosaurs begin to lumber clumsily back across the swamp. And then *Phlegmosaurus* moves. He darts over the swamp on his strong back legs, the forelegs held in close to the muscle-bound trunk, and the great tail jutting stiffly behind, a sort of rudder, or stabilizer, to his crouched and fast-moving body. His head seems all jaw, champing and roaring as he comes. He has selected his prey, a plump young calf, slower than the rest, which now whinnies pitifully for the protection of the herd, a protection that is, in this extremity, forgone. *Phlegmosaurus* is quickly upon the creature. Nimbly avoiding the lashings and thrashings of the brontosaur's great tail, he closes with it and in one bound clamps himself to its shoulder. Up comes a hind leg, and that terrible curved claw glints for an instant in the sunlight—and then in a blur of flying mud and flailing flesh the claw goes slicing again and again at the throat of the brontosaur, and the huge creature sinks with a dreadful wheezing sound into the ooze, and great gouts of blood come pumping from its torn throat. Then, still roaring with fury, *Phlegmosaurus* begins tearing at the dying animal, pulling at the flank until a huge piece of steaming flesh comes away; and for some minutes this frenzy continues, as the brontosaur lies kicking and dying in a muddy pool of its own blood. The rest of the herd has disappeared into the forest, and from the trees there has now arisen a cacophony of shrieks and cries and wild chatterings, and already, at the edge of the swamp, scavengers are beginning to assemble. At last the young herbivore lies still, and the frenzy of ripping and tearing subsides. For some time *Phlegmosaurus* eats methodically, clutching the meat with its forelegs, cutting and slicing with its great claws. Every few moments the head is lifted, and turned this way and that, the jaws dripping gore. Then, when the sun is high overhead, and flooding the swamp with heat and light, the beast slumps onto the ripped corpse and dozes there in the warm dead flesh. Over on the edge of the swamp, from out of its tree trunk, the hairy little mammal once more emerges. Sitting up pertly on its hind legs, it wipes its whiskery snout with both paws, gazing with bright keen eyes at the now-slumbering dinosaur.

Suddenly a ragged scream shatters the stillness of the swamp—and I awoke. I had a moment of confusion, thinking I was still out there, and then with a shock I realized that the scream had come from Cleo's bedroom—she sleeps in the east wing too. Pausing only for my dressing gown and slippers I made my way to her bedside. The poor child was extremely distressed. I found her sitting hunched in bed with her face in her palms. Her curtains were slightly open, and the moonlight that came sifting through the gap spread a pool of illumination on her bed, and in the center of this pool she sat in a white nightgown, weeping. I went to her and she immediately buried her face in my shoulder and clutched me tightly. Huge sobs contorted her thin, trembling frame, and she was quite unable to speak. I held her for several minutes until the sobs slowly subsided and she regained control of herself. At last she lifted her head from my shoulder and I gave her a handkerchief. "Thank you Daddy," she sniffed. "Oh dear," she said. "Oh how horrible. Oh how ghastly."

"What, darling?" I murmured, stroking her hair.

"Oh Daddy," she said—and gazed at me for a long moment from bleary, tear-damp eyes—"oh Daddy, he came to see me again—and it was horrible, much worse than last time."

"*Who* came to see you, darling?" I said, still softly stroking her hair.

"Sidney did, Daddy."

"*Sidney!* That's impossible, darling! Do you mean Sidney is in this house?" I looked over my shoulder, as if Sidney might be lurking in Cleo's closet, or crouching out of sight at the end of the bed.

"No, he's not here, Daddy, you won't see him." She dropped her eyes and sniffed loudly several times. Then up came her face, stark with horror and grief. "He's dead, you see." This provoked a fresh flood of tears.

Slowly, then, the story came out. It seems that this was the second time that Sidney had come to Cleo in the night. These "visits," she insisted, were not dreams: she distinctly remembered awakening. The first time he had been standing beside her bed, and his skin, she said, was chalk-white, translucent, and tinged with a faintly greenish hue. He smelled unpleasantly sweet, said Cleo. He was wearing the suit he'd been in the night he disappeared, a beige tweed affair, jacket and plus fours, with a faint check pattern in yellow and sky-blue. What had riveted her attention, however, was the great ragged angry gash beneath his chin: Sidney had had his throat cut.

Apparently he spoke to her; she did not remember his words exactly; she had been in a state of shock throughout, and could concentrate only on the blackly clotted flap where his neck had once been. But his purpose, it seems, was to warn her. Warn her about what? About the "evil creeping thing" that prowled the countryside after dark. More than this he did not say, that first time. But this time, said Cleo, this time . . . She shuddered violently. "His *voice*, Daddy," she whispered. "He's lost his cords. He's hoarse, like an old man. He doesn't say words, he wheezes them out in this dreadful whisper. And he tells me things."

I took the girl's hands in my own. Speaking very quietly, very gently, I said: "What things, darling?"

"He says the creature that tore out his throat came from this house."

I said nothing. She gazed at me with wide and terrified eyes. "Daddy," she whispered, "it must be Fledge."

I gave her some scotch (I keep a bottle in my bedroom) and managed to settle her down. I sat for some time beside her bed, and watched her as she slept—peacefully now, thank God. I lit a cigar, and by the light of a candle I pondered her strange disclosure about Fledge. So she, too, had intuited his evil. What did this signify? I pondered this question into the small hours, but reached no satisfactory conclusions.

I WAS STILL pondering it when, the next day, as I sat in a bathful of tepid water, I shouted for Fledge to come and scrub my back. I was not yet aware that part of his campaign to usurp me involved the seduction of Harriet, though in retrospect, piecing it all together from my wheelchair, I would guess that by this time—we were now in late January—Harriet had already been to see her priest. And I've no doubt he proscribed the thing on pain of hellfire and damnation. Clearly it wasn't enough. "But I am a woman!" cried Harriet. "You are God's child," the priest replied. "My marriage has been a travesty!" she wailed. "Then you must offer it up as a sacrifice," he said. She came away unconvinced, though perhaps she did not admit this to herself. Something was awakened in her that would not be easily stifled. When Fledge next touched her, she repulsed him, but weakly. He knew she would soon succumb.

Yes, I knew my Harriet, and I knew she would require a period of soul-searching before she abandoned herself to the affair. When, I wonder, did that actually occur? Perhaps it had already happened, and I, preoccupied with my work and, when in the house, with Fledge, failed to notice a change in her. Or perhaps—and this I think more likely—it didn't happen until later, while I was in hospital. "Harder, Fledge," I said—he was scrubbing my back with a piece of coral, and I liked to get the skin red and tingling with the friction, makes one feel marvelously alive. "That's better," I said, as he started to put some muscle into it. Was this not foolhardy, you say, making myself so vulnerable to a man who had killed once already? No, it would have been foolhardy if I had suddenly forbidden him entry to my bathroom; then he would have guessed that I *knew*, and *that* would have been dangerous. Fledge felt secure, he felt that no one suspected him; and this was the way I wanted him to feel.

I climbed out of the bath and stood dripping and shivering on the mat as he rubbed me down with a towel. I wonder, now, what he thought as he performed this service. Did he realize, for instance, just how pleasant it is to be scrubbed and toweled by one's manservant? Was he seething inwardly with resentment that it was I, and not he, who was in a position to order such a toweling? No, I'm more inclined to think that he was filled with a sort of cold certainty that within a few months it would all be different, that he would be the master of Crook, and that I would be—dead. Nor was this the first time that I'd contemplated the fact that

Fledge undoubtedly intended to murder me; and knowing this, but knowing also that he himself did not know that I knew it, I experienced that inimitable tingle, that *frisson*, that a brave man feels in the presence of real danger. "That's enough, Fledge," I said. "Give me my dressing gown." My wiry little body shivered for a moment in that bleak chilly bathroom in the east wing. Turning toward the mirror I noted with pleasure the redness of my hard-scrubbed back, then slipped my arms into the dressing gown that Fledge held open for me. Tying the cord tightly about my waist I told him to bring me a scotch while I dressed for dinner, then along the corridor I went, leaving him to pick up the damp towels and clean out the bathtub. The point is, there was a period when I felt stimulated by the challenge Fledge represented, by the vigor of the conflict he offered. As I dressed I thought with a dry snort that he was a fool to imagine he could outwit me. Events, however, were soon to occur that gave him the advantage; and these events were beyond my control, they originated with that meddling old woman, Giblet.

The early part of February was very damp in our part of the country, and it was also, as I've said, a very busy and nerve-wracking time for me. For quite apart from the complex and delicate, and deadly serious, game I was playing with Fledge, I was also preparing to deliver my lecture on the seventh. So I was in the barn every day, rehearsing the thing to a group of shrouded bones and a raucous crow that had roosted in the rafters. I'd had to shroud *Phlegmosaurus*, in tarpaulins and old sheets, because the roof leaked and the rain dripped through. I paced up and down, reciting my revolutionary thesis on the taxonomic classification of the dinosaur and reveling, I admit, in my imagination, in the storm of applause and controversy I expected to arouse. I expected, frankly, soon to be dominating the discourse of natural history—or at least its paleontological strand—I, the gentleman naturalist, the amateur! I intended, you see, to take my audience slowly and carefully through the fossil record, from bottom to top, showing how the first primitive reptiles were succeeded by the advanced ''reptiles''—dinosaurs with birdlike bodies—after which came primitive birds with teeth, like *Archaeopteryx*, then advanced birds with teeth, then modern toothless birds. I would show how the bone structure of *Phlegmosaurus*, and his upright, bipedal posture, are distinctly avian, and I would *not* accept the argument that because he had lost the large collarbone required by all flying birds his relationship to the birds was therefore a distant one. No, I would suggest that the *potential* for growing a collarbone was still there in the phlegmosaurian genes, but dormant, simply. I would suggest that as my *Phlegmosaurus* went darting across the Mesozoic landscape, he reached high enough speeds to become airborne. I would suggest that natural selection would then favor any mutation through which his long-suppressed collarbone reappeared. And this reappearance of suppressed characteristics—*atavisms*, we call them—are not as uncommon as you might think. Whales with legs occasionally turn up, as do horses with toes. Such throwbacks even occur in our own species: babies with tails, for instance. By way of the atavism, then, I would show that *Phlegmosaurus carbonensis* grew a collarbone, sprouted feathers, and took to the air. He was thus the father of the birds, and not to be classed among the reptiles.

Harriet, I remember, was showing signs that my fouler-than-usual mood was beginning to irritate her. She has a remarkably high tolerance for mean-spirited unsociability, but there is a limit; and the peevish frown crinkling her brow indicated to me that her threshold would shortly be reached. I should have told her that after the lecture I'd be a changed man, but I didn't feel up to it. It occurs to me now, though, that perhaps her uncharacteristic ill-humor was not related to my behavior at all, but was, rather, a symptom of the struggle going on in her own heart; for in Harriet the spirit and the flesh were at war at this time, I'm convinced.

Cleo was no help. She wouldn't eat with us, she wouldn't let Harriet into her room, and she absolutely refused to go back to Oxford. I should have told Harriet not to worry, that it would "blow over," like the rain (all emotion is like weather, I think: if you wait long enough it passes), but I didn't feel up to that either, I was much too engrossed in my own drama. Doris was still functional; Fledge was inscrutable. This was Crook, then, as the rain kept falling on its moss-infested tiles and even came dripping through, in places, especially at the back of the house, where buckets had to be placed on landings and stairwells to catch the drips. It was Fledge's job to empty them; I saw him one morning, a bucket in each hand, coming down the back stairs, and it made me think of George, off to feed the pigs. The contrast between the two men could not have been stronger, I remember thinking, though oddly enough, if one were to strip them naked, tear off the uniform of social identity, as it were, the difference would not, I think, be nearly so pronounced. In terms of bone structure and general physical build they were quite similar. They might even have been brothers, strange thought.

And all the while Mrs. Giblet was out on the marsh, searching for signs of upheaval, a bone in the mud to set her mind at rest about her missing child. It made people uneasy. Old John Crowthorne told me about it in the Hodge and Purlet one afternoon, then spat in the fire. Anyone who knows John Crowthorne will tell you what it means when he spits in the fire. The rain did not deter her, apparently; she was out there in the wettest weather beneath a huge black umbrella, squelching through the mire. Each evening she ate alone at the back of the saloon bar, but fortunately she did not appear while I was there. I slept very badly; I may have had more dreams; I never remembered them in the morning, however. The Fling flooded its banks near Pock and carried off a sheep.

There was nothing, as far as I can remember, to indicate that February 5 would be such a crucial day in these unfolding events. Perhaps the signs were there, the omens and portents, and I was blind to them. My empiricism was more or less intact then, and maybe that was what rendered me blind to warnings. I was drinking whisky in the barn at half-past two in the afternoon when Fledge came in and delivered a message: Mrs. Giblet had succeeded, she had found Sidney's bones. The news alarmed me deeply—I was thinking of Cleo, of course, and what this terrible development would mean to her.

IN RETROSPECT IT was, I suppose, not so much the finding of the bones that alarmed me as it was the state in which they came up. You see, I have dug up quite enough bones in my time to visualize clearly the scene out there on the marsh, though of course I have always dug up dry bones, and these were damp. But the patient labor of exposure and retrieval, with this I am deeply familiar. Mrs. Giblet apparently stumbled upon a piece of rib—this was more than a mile from where the bicycle had come up—a piece of rib that the earth was in the process of disgorging. By means of a small gardening trowel that she carried on her person she then uncovered the entire rib cage, and, close by, the skull. As I say, I am no stranger to such activity. But when I heard that the skeleton continued to come up piecemeal, bone by bone—and that there were *teeth-*

marks on the bones—it was then that I became truly alarmed. For (*experto crede*) it sounded to me very much as though Sidney had been chopped into pieces before being dumped in the marsh, and that in the meanwhile someone, or something, had chewed him clean of flesh and gristle. In other words, he had been butchered, and then gnawed.

Butchered and gnawed. Limp and his men were soon on the marsh, and by dint of energetic excavation had the entire skeleton up by nightfall. The grisly remains were then rushed to the forensic laboratories for analysis, and speculation, in the hours that followed, was intense, not to say macabre. The lab report came the following morning, and did little to allay my fears: Sidney had indeed been butchered and gnawed—butchered by men and gnawed by pigs!

The vague unease I'd been feeling since the bones came up now took definite form, for I quickly understood the implications of this. That it was a piece of typical police bungling I was in no doubt, no doubt at all; but you see, the pig farm in Ceck's Bottom—*my* pig farm—was the only pig farm in the vicinity of the Ceck Marsh, and it was not hard to predict what Limp would do next.

I was in the public bar of the Hodge and Purlet on the evening of the sixth, and there I met old John Crowthorne. That afternoon, he told me, just as he'd been crossing the farmyard with a bucket of swill in each hand, two police cars had come racing through the gate and squelched to a halt on the dung-puddled stones (it was rather a wet and overcast afternoon). Limp leaped out of the first car. "George Lecky?" he shouted.

"No," said old John, who I've no doubt presented a most unwholesome aspect to the bustling little police inspector, for he sports a pair of huge brown whiskers and his face is deeply grooved down the vertical, and each groove seems to be full of earth. "No," he said, as large policemen clambered out of the cars.

"You are?" said Limp.

"John Crowthorne. Afternoon, Hubert," he said, addressing Cleggie, the Ceck policeman.

"Where is George Lecky?" demanded Limp; then, without waiting for an answer: "Right, we're going to search the farm. We have a warrant"—and, turning to his men: "In you go!"

Standing in the public bar, listening to all this, I became very annoyed. This business of pigs gnawing Sidney's bones—this, as I say, was a lot of rot. And that that officious little bastard Limp should go down to the pig farm—*my* property, don't forget, it still belonged to the Crook estate—and start searching the place, and carting off George's tools, his knives and saws and choppers, as old John told me—it was not to be borne. "Good Christ," I muttered, tossing my cigar into the fire, "the nerve of that bloody little man!"

Old John's eyes narrowed, and he glanced at me shrewdly. Odd, this, considering that old John's eyes tend to dart constantly about the walls and ceilings of any room he's in, some sort of nervous tic, I suppose. He turned briefly toward the fire, and spat a large gob of saliva into the flames; there was a brief hiss. Then he told me what happened next, and quite dramatic it was too. Just after they'd loaded a pile of blood-caked sacking into one of the police cars there came a sudden great roaring sound from over by the marsh, and through the murk could be seen a huge shining eye, moving at speed down the Ceck's Bottom road in the direction of the farm. Limp and the constables apparently stood as if rooted to the stones as this one-eyed thing came lurching and backfiring into the farmyard— it was George, of course, at the wheel of the swill lorry. He came careering into the yard, swinging the lorry in a wide U-turn that forced them all up against the walls, and knowing the condition of that lorry, and the size of the yard, I can well imagine how he must have dragged at the wheel and stamped madly at the foot pedals to pull off such a maneuver. Then, said old John, he went reeling and roaring by, and then he was rattling out of the farmyard, still backfiring loudly, and away up the Ceck's Bottom road toward the village. A faint smell of petrol and burning oil hung in the air; porcine grunting continued, basso profundo, in the background. "It were like he cast a spell on us, the way he come round the yard like that," said old John, his voice lowered and his eyes bright. "The odd thing seem, Sir Hugo, that I seen his face as he come by me, and he were *afraid*, were George, he were in a *panic*!" Limp apparently broke the spell. "Right!" he shouted. "Into the cars! Let's get after him!"—and beneath the bemused gaze of old John Crowthorne the police cars raced out of the farmyard, sirens wailing, in pursuit of George.

The Ceck's Bottom road is not ideally suited for high-speed car chases. It is rutted and potholed and strewn with boulders and dung and the occasional stray cow. They never did catch up to George; by the time they reached Ceck the quarry had long since been lost sight of. Into the Hodge and Purlet ran Limp—this I heard from Bill Cudlip, who was there at the time—then out again. "Back the way we came!" he shouted. "He must have gone into the marsh!" Hearty chortles, by the way, from Crowthorne and Cudlip at the ease with which George had shaken off his pursuers, and privately I, too, exulted. George had indeed gone into the marsh, they found his vehicle halfway down the cart track, and I can imagine the headlights of the police car picking out the filthy mudguards, the swill-crusted tailgate, the ranked dustbins on the bed of the familiar lorry. Beyond the channel of the headlights, however, the trees heaved up in a black and impenetrable wall. They would then have got out of the cars and stood listening to the marsh, which stretched for miles beyond the trees, a dark and treacherous tract of land that a man would be a fool to enter after dark, unless he knew it well. A deep silence lay upon the place. "Let him run," murmured Limp. "I'll have fifty men out here in the morning."

But Limp's fifty men failed to find George, though they searched the marsh quite thoroughly, and quite systematically, for several days. That night, though, the night of the sixth, I stood gazing into the fire and thought of my old friend George, at that very moment somewhere out on the Ceck Marsh, fleeing the law. Why? What had he done? What had he to be afraid of? A terrible suspicion begin to take shape in some dark corner of my mind—no, I would not heed it, I pushed it down—no, not that.

I AM SITTING *not* in my grotto under the stairs as I tell you this, but in the kitchen, with Doris and Cleo, having my fingernails clipped. It is mid-April, and I have been back from the hospital for more than a month. I spend most of my time in the kitchen now; Cleo is still far from well, but at least she's not brooding in the east wing anymore; she, too, now spends her days hanging round the kitchen, and thus a sort of splitting has occurred in Crook, a sort of crisp demarcation between the front of the house and the back, with Harriet and Fledge at one end and Doris and Cleo at the other, and myself as a neutral term that goes wheeling back and forth between the two like a tennis ball. So I sit here enjoying the sunshine, and the attention of Doris and Cleo, and try to construct for you as full and coherent an account as I can of *how things got this way*.

You must forgive me if I appear at times to contradict myself, or in other ways violate the natural order of the events I am disclosing; this business of selecting and organizing one's memories so as to describe precisely *what happened* is a delicate, perilous undertaking, and I'm beginning to wonder whether it may not be beyond me. The scientific attitude to which I have for decades been faithful, with its strict notions of objectivity, etc., has come under heavy assault since the accident. Cracks have appeared, and from out of those cracks grin monstrous anomalies. I cannot subdue them. I have become superstitious. I am subject to "sightings."

I suppose I shall have to describe the circumstances surrounding the accident sooner or later. Frankly, I would rather do it later; the whole incident still causes me intense embarrassment and pain, because Fledge, you see, was present when it occurred, he was instrumental, in fact, in causing it. I shall render a full account of all this in due course. Suffice for now that after I regained consciousness I went through a very morbid period indeed, for it is terrifying to will to move and remain inert, and it is terrifying to experience the sense of disorder this inertia produces. And although in time I began to negotiate some sort of commerce with objective reality, to *adapt*, during my first days in hospital I was afflicted by, of all things, a sense of failure. I would lie in the darkness, trapped in the dungeon of my own skull, which throbbed like a jackhammer, and I would strain with every fiber of my being just to lift the little finger of my right hand. I threw all my resources into lifting that pinky a tenth of an inch off the bedsheet. This would intensify my headache to the point that I expected my head quite literally to explode, but the damn pinky *would not move*, and after some minutes I would be seized, first, with the utmost sense of despair and futility, and then with shame at my own failure. This was in the early days, as I say, before I began actively to accept that I was *a man without a body*. Later of course I came to terms with my condition. This was not courage but instinct, pure instinct, the will to survive, and I share it with all living organisms. There was, though, this period when it seemed to me that if I never moved again it would be my own fault, because I had not tried hard enough. Strange how reluctant I was to acknowledge that control of my fate lay beyond my own conscious will. Habit of a lifetime, I suppose.

Oh, but the back door is open, the birds are singing, and the sunshine of the afternoon is puddling warmly on the old gray stones. It is springtime now, and the damp days of that awful February are behind us. Cleo, I notice, is indulging a bizarre new hobby of hers, collecting nail clippings in a matchbox, and Doris, who is operating the scissors, pauses now and then to sip her sherry. A scene of pleasant domestic tranquillity, then, and frankly it's hard for me to keep my mind on gnawed bones and dismembered corpses. "Now your toenails," says Cleo, and the pair of them get down on their hands and knees to remove my shoes and socks. I derive enormous pleasure from this ritual, indeed from any situation in which I am physically touched, though feeling their fingers on my feet is ticklish, and I should giggle like a child if I were capable of it. "What smelly feet you've got, Daddy,'' says Cleo. ''Like a pair of old cheddars, aren't they, Mrs. Fledge?''

Doris is giving me her lopsided smile. Dear Doris, I would much rather think about her than about dead Sidney and his pig-gnawed bones. Doris for me is the source of life now. She feeds me. She washes me. She changes me, she dresses me. She coos and burbles over me like the fondest young mother. And I, devoid of any other physical contact with the world, have come to crave and adore the touch of her hands on my body, I have come to love everything about the woman, even the smell of drink on her breath and the intoxicated fumblings of the night. I cry sometimes when I am with Doris, when she handles me tenderly in the bathroom or the lavatory, but it never occurs to her, as it has to Cleo, that crying should be impossible for a vegetable. This is because she does not see me as others see me, in terms of my brain damage. I am her baby.

Dear Doris. I haven't told you about my return to Crook; it could hardly be called triumphant. My condition had apparently ''stabilized''—''fossilized,'' I should have said. I could sit in a wheelchair, masticate and swallow, defecate, weep—and that, in terms of physical activity, was it. I had an alarming tendency to grind my teeth, and sometimes my breathing would become heavily labored—I would *snore*, in fact, while wide awake. I noticed that this snoring occurred when I thought about painful topics, like Fledge, and hence I would snore much of the day, though in sleep, apparently, I was quiet. (Such reversals were common, in my life as a vegetable.) At moments of vivid emotion the snores would become increasingly strained and build towards a crescendo of honks and grunts, at which point I would be forced to abandon thought altogether and concentrate hard on bringing my respiration back under control; nurses would run over to clap me violently on the back. It was this phenomenon that provoked Walter Dendrite, my neurologist, to refer to me publicly as a pig. But the point is, Doris volunteered to look after the snorting monster I had become; she agreed to perform the services of a mother to me, and for this I love her.

Harriet and Hilary traveled back to Crook with me in the ambulance. Harriet no longer burst into tears every time she laid eyes on me, the doctors had seen to that, I'd heard them murmuring at the foot of my bed. In fact, it was one of the most striking aspects of that first stage of my vegetal existence, the experience of seeing my family's reactions shift from grief and compassion to acceptance and apparent indifference in a remarkably short period of time. Thus, I notice, are the dead forgotten; thus are persons in my state rendered tolerable. For who can look long upon a creature whose one stark message is: see how close *you* are to grotesquerie. Our kinship with the grotesque is something to be shunned; it requires an act of rejection, of brisk alienation, and here the doctors were most cooperative, for they permitted Harriet and the rest of them to reject my persisting humanity by means of a gobbledygook that carried the imprimatur of—science! Science! And this is not the least of the ironies with which this tale of mine is so liberally peppered—science proposes, this is how I had lived, but science also *dis*poses, and now I found myself frozen, stuck fast, like a fly in a web, in the grid of a medical taxonomy. My identity was now neuropathological. I was no longer a man, I was an instance of a disease, and as such I could no longer arouse the profound pity I so richly deserved. I don't think they gave me very long to live, frankly. They knew about my ticker and its sclerotic arteries. I imagine if I'd been an Eskimo they'd just have pushed me out into a blizzard, and that would have been that. I wouldn't have minded, or rather, I wouldn't have minded if I could have taken Fledge out into the blizzard with me. Then I'd have died a happy man. Did I mention that the appalling Patrick Pin had been hovering at my bedside when I regained consciousness? It seems that Harriet, fearing for my life, had had him administer Extreme Unction. That was not all: I now sported a small crucifix on a silver chain around my neck. I would be safe from vampires, in any event. Ha!

But the point is, my return to Crook was remarkable for what it taught me about the nature of *hope*. Bear with me, please, the pertinence of these remarks will soon become clear. Fledge, you see, had wheeled me from the ambulance to the house, and down the hall to the drawing room, and as he'd done so it had been impossible not to be aware of a quite sickening aura of triumphalism that clung to the man like a smell, that seeped malodorously from all his wretched pores. He put me against the wall, facing the fireplace, and left me there.

Now Crook, as Sidney's mother had so astutely remarked to Harriet on New Year's Eve, is a house of wood; and despite the fact that it is falling down, it retains strong character precisely because it *is* wood.

The staircase and all the floorboards are of oak, as is the wall paneling, which is dark, and makes the rooms snug and warm. The doorframes are also wood, and have a lovely shallow arch to them, delicately cusped at the center. The front door is divided into studded panels, but decoration is otherwise limited to the tops of the wall panels and the downstairs skirting boards. Around the chimneypiece in the drawing room, however—and my wheelchair, as I say, had been placed so that I gazed directly at it—there is some very elaborate work. It is in fact a masterpiece, a masterpiece of Tudor low-relief carving.

A pair of oak columns flank the fireplace, supporting an entablature, or superstructure, comprising architrave, frieze, and cornice. The projection of the latter forms the mantelpiece, and upon it the design of the entire fireplace is repeated, though naturally in greatly reduced proportions. There is thus an *echo* upon the mantelpiece of the whole fireplace—can you picture it?—and whereas the space between the lower columns is the open grate itself, in the carving above are displayed the arms of the Coal family (Chimaera, salient, gules on sable) and beneath them our motto: *NIL DESPERANDUM*.

Nil desperandum. Since I was a boy I've felt that those words were meant for me. At times of crisis—in Africa, for instance—they have given me strength. It's surprising, is it not, how much solace can be had from two words—literally, "there is no reason to despair"? Perhaps they matter so much to me because I have a very real tendency to despair. It runs in the family: Sir Digby Coal was a suicide, and Cleo, I'm very much afraid, appears also to have a melancholy cast of mind; along with the teeth she gets it from me. But for four centuries the words over the fireplace, standing, perhaps, in allegorical relation to the fire beneath, have helped my forebears to struggle against their innate inclination to give up hope. These words have warmed their souls, while the flames beneath have warmed their bones. There is a way, I have come to believe, that a structure, in time, becomes immanent with the spirit of its residents, and to this also I may have been responding when I gazed at the chimneypiece that morning. Strange sentiments for a scientist, you say. But as I think is becoming clear, I was by this time losing my grip on the sternly empirico-mechanist view of Nature to which I had for years been faithful.

Well, as I gazed at the chimneypiece, at the coat-of-arms and, below it, our motto, something totally unexpected occurred. Something stirred within me, and I felt a brief surge of exaltation. Those immortal words over the fireplace, you see, reminded me that *I was a Coal*, and that *I would not be bested by a servant*. Completely unwittingly, Fledge had provided me the one single stimulus that was guaranteed to brace and hearten me—and for the first time since the accident I felt the spirit move within me. Perhaps, indeed, I suddenly thought, there really was no reason to despair. From what I had heard in the hospital, the doctors had no confidence in my ever regaining the use of my body, but I decided, there and then, to hope all the same, and within the fossil of my frozen frame something took fire and blazed.

Yes, coming back to Crook revived and reinvigorated

me, and so it was, after all, a sort of triumph. As I think back on it now, I remember being shocked at first at the racket my wheelchair made on the old wooden floorboards, how it had rumbled and thundered down the hall, me at the helm with my prowlike nose jutting forward and my old claws clamped on the arms of the thing; but I remember too how, after a moment or so, the shock had been replaced by a grim delight that my progress about my house would be such a noisy business, that my movement would be signaled so loudly and emphatically to all within earshot by this thunder of wheels on boards. Then, too, I was in my tweeds again. I had shrunk in hospital, they were ill-fitting now, but they were *my* tweeds, my hairy tweeds, with leather patches on the elbows and thick flaps on the pockets so that nothing could fall out. It was a suit that had been made for me by a firm of London tailors who catered exclusively to the country gentleman, and who had dressed my father, and his father before him. (They have since gone out of business, sadly.) But all these things helped to revive me from that awful torpor to which my month in hell had reduced me. And while not a hint, not a flicker, of any of this was apparent in my posture or expression, there was, within, a sort of life-affirming celebration under way. *Nil desperandum*, Hugo, I told myself, *nil desperandum*, old chap.

OH GOOD GOD, I've drifted far ahead of myself. My chronology is all skewed again. Where am I?

George Lecky had gone into the Ceck Marsh, and Limp's men had been unable to find him. Nothing strange about this; George had lived close to the marsh for twenty-five years, ever since I'd brought him back from Africa with me, and he probably knew that drear tract better than any man in Berkshire, with the exception of old John Crowthorne. So it would not have been hard for him to evade the constabulary out there. But I was not surprised when, three days later, he appeared in my barn. Actually I'd been expecting him—who else would he go to but his old African comrade?

I was sitting in my wicker chair, gazing at *Phlegmosaurus*, when I became aware of movement in the roof. I looked up; he was standing at the top of the staircase to the loft, his head bathed in a pool of wintry sunlight from the little window in the gable behind him, so that his features were entirely masked by shadow. For a moment neither of us spoke, neither of us moved. It was an important moment, a sort of test. I did not hesitate. Rising from my chair, and extending my arms upward toward him, I cried: "Well good God man, come down. You must be starving!"

I embraced my old comrade warmly, despite the smell. A man who has been living rough in the Ceck Marsh for several days is not in pleasant condition. His jacket and trousers were filthy with mud, still damp on the seat and cuffs, sticks of straw and other plant matter clinging to them. He was bareheaded, unshaven, and foul of breath, and from his features had disappeared that habitually stoic and tranquil expression, replaced now by watchfulness, nervousness, and fear. He had a *hunted* look. I sat him in the wicker chair and gave him some scotch. He took a swallow, then pulled back his lips from his teeth and briefly rubbed his scalp and then his eyes. He drank more whisky. I could sense it heating and reviving him. I gave him a few minutes to compose himself. Should I go to the house for food? No, not yet, he wanted to talk first. He finished the whisky and bent his body forward in the chair, his palms on his knees and his elbows sticking out, his arms thus forming a pair of rigid buttresses to his tense, exhausted frame. He gazed at the floor of the barn and took a series of deep breaths. "So George," I said at last, "what's going on?"

Have I spoken to you of the unreliability of memory?

Retrospection does yield order, no doubt about that, but I wonder if this order isn't perhaps achieved solely as a function of the remembering mind, which of its very nature tends to yield order. I say this only because the conversation that follows occurred a long time ago, and much has happened in the interim. But the *spirit* of that conversation—this I think I have captured, and this is the important thing.

George shook his head. His hand kept going to his neck, where he rubbed it hard against an angry rash, the result of contact with some virulent piece of vegetation out in the marsh, I presume. Clearly the thing itched badly, and I made a mental note to bring ointment with me from the house. Still staring at the floor he began to speak; and he surprised me, for it was John Crowthorne he spoke about, he was abusing the man, calling him an old fool—it had occurred to me that old John might play a part in all this, but I hadn't pursued it very far. George spoke with a low, halting cadence; then up came his head, and he glared at me with an angry but pathetically futile passion, the passion of a man who knows his predicament is intractable and hopeless.

"But what about old John?" I coaxed him. In the silence that followed we could both distinctly hear a rat scuffling through the hay at the far end of the barn. "I gave him the lorry," said George at last, dropping his eyes to the floor, "and he takes it round the back of the marsh." I nodded; old John used George's swill lorry for his more far-ranging nocturnal poaching expeditions, this I knew well. "I didn't hear him when he come back, but something woke me in the night so I

Patrick McGrath

go to the window, and there's a light in the shed. Well, I open the window and I *hear* it."

Another silence. "Hear what, George?" I said softly. I gave him more scotch.

He rubbed his neck. "Someone chopping in there. I could hear someone chopping in there. So I go down."

I nodded again; when George mentioned the shed, it was his slaughterhouse he was referring to. "I go down," he said. His voice had become blank of emotion, hollow, as though unable to admit to comprehension of what he was saying. "I go down," he repeated. "I can hear him in there as I cross the yard; he's chopping something. 'That you, John?' I say, when I'm at the door. He's at the back and he's chopping something up. He turns round, grinning at me like a bloody monkey."

George fell silent again. His eyes were wide as he stared at the floor. "He didn't know who it was," he muttered, and a terrible understanding dawned upon me, and as George stared at the floor the barn seemed to grow suddenly very dark, and in my own mind I could hear that terrible chopping in the night, the terrible chopping that woke George from sleep, and I could see old John grinning in the gloom of the shed as he chopped up what he'd found out on the marsh. "He didn't know who it was," whispered George, and there was horror in his voice. "He found him out on the marsh in a sack, and since it weren't a local man, he says to himself, I'll let the pigs have him." Silence again; George dropped his head, set his elbows on his knees, and again rubbed his neck. "I took the chopper from him," he muttered, "but it was too late."

156

"Too late?"

Another long pause. George didn't answer; it hardly mattered, I'd guessed his meaning. "I wanted to knock him down, I was that furious," he muttered. His voice had a faraway sound to it now, as though it came from the end of a very long tunnel. "Wouldn't have done no good." Another silence; the crow stirred in the rafters overhead, then flapped noisily to another perch a few feet higher in the roof. I rose from my chair and again paced the barn; I was now all too clear about what had happened. Just as I'd speculated on Christmas night, someone had disturbed Fledge out on the marsh, and found Sidney's body in a sack. That someone was old John Crowthorne. "Just had to finish the job," George murmured, a little later, "that's all there was to it." Then he looked up and said in a clear, firm voice: "It was old John buried the bones, when the pigs was done. Didn't do a very good job of it, eh? Eh?" George laughed, a terrible laugh, hopeless and black. "Made a bloody awful job of it, didn't he? Oh good Christ"— and he clenched his fists tight, closed his eyes, and pulled back the lips from his teeth in that terrible grimace. A single harsh screech came from the rafters, and again the clumsy flap of wings.

I said nothing more for some minutes. I had come round to the back of George's chair. I gripped him by the shoulders and squeezed them warmly. I understood his predicament; he would never go to the police with this story; for one thing, he had worked beside old John Crowthorne almost as long as he'd been in Ceck, and besides, his own complicity was clear. But I put it to him anyway, and as I expected he was adamant. He was a countryman, and he had all the countryman's suspicion of police and officials and institutions; he followed natural law, but the ghastly irony at the heart of all this was that so did John Crowthorne. I told him he should stay in the barn while we tried to think the thing through. Then I went over to the house to get bread and cheese for him, and ointment for the rash on his neck.

Crossing the driveway I began to see a net of guilt, a net that originated with Fledge, that had enmeshed old John Crowthorne, and then George, and now me too, inasmuch as I was shielding George from the law. As I entered the house Fledge was emerging from the drawing room. The effect of seeing *him*, *then*, was strong, but I attempted not to show it. He followed me down to the kitchen and began to prepare Harriet's tea tray. "Have we any ointment, Fledge?" I said, after fetching out a loaf of bread and some cheddar.

"Ointment, Sir Hugo?"

"Yes, ointment," I snapped. "Salve, embrocation—something to soothe a rash. Oh never mind," I said, "I'll find it myself." I'd suddenly realized how precarious George's situation was; it would be extremely unwise to let Fledge know he was here. I left the kitchen to look for ointment, conscious of the butler's curious eyes upon me as he laid the tray for Harriet's afternoon tea.

I returned to the barn and found George still sitting in the wicker chair with his head in his hands. The light was fading by this time, and the shadows had begun to cluster about him. He sat across from *Phlegmosaurus*, and an oddly dramatic tableau they made, the heavy-jawed skeleton rearing over the rigid figure in the wicker chair. He ate ravenously and drank more whisky, but first he rubbed the ointment I'd brought him into the rash, which extended, I now saw, almost all the way round his neck. "In a bloody sack," he muttered as he ate. "Who done him, tell me that? Who put him out there in a sack like that?"

I hesitated to tell him. I frowned. I rose from my chair and turned on the lights. "No," cried George, lifting a hand to his eyes. "Leave them off!" I turned them off and returned to my chair. George had finished eating. He wiped his hand across his mouth and glared at me. He was stronger for having eaten, much stronger. "Who done him, Sir Hugo? You know. Tell me."

Still I hesitated. Would it, I wondered, be to George's advantage to know what I knew? I was aware of an indefinite feeling of deep unease at the prospect of telling George the truth. "Tell me," he said.

"All right, George," I said, and I told him. He listened in silence. When I had finished he said he wanted to smoke, I only had cigars, so I gave him one of those. Still he made no comment on what I had told him. His mind was busy, however, and suddenly I glimpsed the old George, the tough and taciturn man I knew so well, the man who kept his own counsel. The food, the drink, the shelter of my gloomy barn—these things had dispelled the fear that he had acquired in the marsh. Soon, I knew, he would take his destiny in his own hands once more. What did this mean for me? For Fledge? Suddenly I felt great dread, as I felt control of the situation slipping through my fingers. George and I sat smoking as the barn grew darker, and all I could see of him then was a brooding, silent, shadowy phantom, hunched around the glowing red tip of a cigar.

George slept in the barn that night, up in the loft among the stored bones, and the next night also, and he continued to grow stronger. And as he grew stronger, so did he grow more silent, and if he formed a plan of some sort, he did not communicate it to me. I quickly came to regret having told him about Fledge. I began to think that he should give himself up, and regardless of his scruples tell the police what he knew. This would mean involving me, and Fledge too, of course. It would be extremely tiresome for the family, particularly for Cleo, but after all there *had* been murder committed. George would have to serve time in prison, and Fledge would swing. Or would he? I had no confidence that this was so. All I had were my suspicions, my convictions, but nothing in the way of hard, incontrovertible, empirical *fact*. Perhaps George would simply put his own head in the noose, if he went to the police—his own or John Crowthorne's. Could old John be persuaded to go to the police? Unlikely. That old poacher was deeply deficient in the moral sense, this was clear; this was a man who could find a body in a sack and, because "it weren't a local man," cheerfully butcher it for pig feed. But George would never betray him, this I knew; for I had had ample opportunity, over the years, to observe how deep the loyalty ran in George Lecky, once he was committed to a man. For twenty-five years, you see, George had been fiercely, discreetly, and uncompromisingly loyal to *me*.

Two days and two nights George stayed in the barn. Limp's men were still out on the marsh looking for him, though according to the papers his description had been circulated throughout the southeast, suggesting that the police now considered it at least possible that he'd left the area. The atmosphere in the house was tense, not least because I was being impossible. For quite apart from the strain I was experiencing hiding George, I had also to assimilate what was probably the single most humiliating event of my scientific career.

For I had, indeed, delivered my lecture on the seventh, I'd delivered it to an audience of four: Hilary, Victor, Sykes-Herring, and a man called Sir Edward Cleghorn. Cleghorn is an eccentric crank; he is Harriet's "pterodactyl man," and he claims that he and I are the only gentlemen naturalists still working in Britain. His presence was frankly an embarrassment. Sykes-Herring was there because he had to be, as, in a way, were Hilary and Victor. Harriet and Cleo had not attended, Sidney's bones having come up only two days before. Two old men blundered in, thinking it a lecture on coprolites, then blundered out again; and that, in terms of what should have been the crowning moment of my paleontological career, was it.

Afterwards, after I had reviewed the dinosaur-bird relationship from evolutionary and anatomical perspective, after I had spoken at length about the phlegmosaurian claw and the phlegmosaurian hipbone, and the implications of said claw and hipbone, after I had thumped the pulpit, like Thomas Huxley, for *Archaeopteryx*, oldest of the fossil birds, after I had talked about atavisms, and stressed the necessity of asking ourselves whether the dinosaur was truly the cold-

blooded reptile we unthinkingly assumed him to be—
after I had said all this, and more, there was the small,
thin sound, in that vast, empty auditorium, of eight
hands clapping. "Very interesting," said Sykes-
Herring, as he took us to tea in the senior common
room. "Most provocative." He didn't believe a word
I'd said. In his own mind he was harrumphing like a
walrus. Cleghorn drew me aside and, spraying me with
cake crumbs and saliva as he spoke, told me I was
wasting my breath. "Can't go meddling with the taxonomy," he said, "terrifies people. It's been this way
since Baron Cuvier, and he died"—here he half-choked
on a piece of cake—"in 1832! Darwin was barely aboard
the *Beagle*!" I could have done without this; Eddy
Cleghorn is extremely unstable, and quite probably
mad. Young Victor was enthusiastic, and this was
something, I suppose. Perhaps he would follow in my
footsteps, revolutionize paleontology. He was, after all,
a Coal. But why, I asked myself, had the professional
scientific community so unanimously ignored me? Was
it, as Cleghorn suggested, because they were made anx-
ious at seeing the established classification of dinosaurs
challenged? "Can't go meddling with the taxonomy,"
the old crank had said. "See what happens to a mis-
shelved book? Ceases to exist. Shake up the order, you
shake up the world. Frightens people, Hugo, believe
me. You're a radical." Bloody fool. I began to suspect,
actually, that the true cause of my humiliation was
Sykes-Herring. I began to suspect that he had failed to
publicize the lecture. No one came, I think, simply because no one knew about it. Once again, it seems, I
was being persecuted. Sykes-Herring had done this be-

fore, you see, in fact he had blighted my entire career, and I now saw that if I was ever to teach the world the phlegmosaurian lesson, I should have to circumvent Sykes-Herring. He was a malevolent, obscurantist reactionary. I should have to be very careful, very *cunning*, if I was going to best him. He was, after all, the Secretary of the Royal Society. Ha! Little did I know that scientific politics would soon be beyond me forever!

IT WAS DIFFICULT, extremely difficult, to resume paleontology after that. In a way, then, it was fortunate that I had George's welfare to occupy me in the days that followed, otherwise I might well have succumbed to depression. For two days and two nights he slept among my bones, growing stronger, emanating a silent purposefulness that made me very uneasy indeed. I tried to talk to him but he would not be drawn. He sat in my wicker chair by the hour, smoking, frowning abstractedly, from time to time stamping a boot on the floor. The house was no less grim. Cleo had reacted to the rising of Sidney's bones by crawling even further into her shell, and to Harriet's distress she never appeared for meals. She was, of course, oppressed by the conviction that Fledge was the evil creeping thing that had murdered Sidney on the marsh, and she bore no small antagonism toward Harriet and myself for continuing to tolerate the man. Harriet told me that if I didn't telephone Henry Horn about the girl soon, then she would. There was, thus, an atmosphere of brooding malevolence in both house and barn, and it very quickly degenerated into a sort of smoldering latent explosiveness.

The only one not directly implicated in any of this was Doris, of course; but she felt it, and quite unconsciously she responded to it. Perhaps the most striking manifestation of this was the raw fish incident.

This occurred at lunchtime on the Friday of that week. We always had fish on Fridays, Harriet being Roman Catholic, and this day we were to be served a nice piece of halibut. Interesting creature, the halibut—*Hippoglossus hippoglossus*, literally, horse-tongue horse-tongue. It begins life upright, one eye on either side of its head, and then in early youth develops the peculiar habit of lying on the bottom of the sea and covering itself with sand. In such a position the eye on the lower side, invariably the left side, cannot serve any useful purpose, so it migrates to the top side, socket and all. Yes, the halibut has a *migrating eye*. A voracious feeder, it consumes all sorts of other fish, an occasional sea bird, and relishes rubbish, like the pig.

But that's not strictly relevant. Fledge set an earthenware casserole dish in front of Harriet, and when she lifted the lid, there lay the piece of halibut, skin, fins, and all—completely raw. It had seen neither knife nor oven; there hadn't even been the *pretense* of cooking it! Harriet is a placid soul, but this roused her. "What on *earth* is the woman up to?" she murmured. And then,

I remember this well, just when one would have expected her to turn to Fledge, and demand an explanation—she did not. She dabbed at her lips with her napkin, rose from her chair, and left the room without another word. There was a moment's silence. "Take it away, Fledge," I said, "and bring the cheeseboard." I presumed Harriet had gone to the kitchen to talk to Doris, but as she never returned to the dining room it occurs to me now that possibly she did not go near the kitchen at all. It occurs to me now that this was as good a demonstration as one could want of *a woman embarrassed in front of her butler*. Had something happened? Had Fledge made another advance and, as I predicted, been repulsed, but weakly? I rather think he had.

Things came to a head that afternoon. George was in the wicker chair; I was striding up and down and attempting to make him tell me what was on his mind. How long did he intend "holing up" in my barn? I demanded. He had to *act*, I told him. I was feeling the strain, myself, and I may have been more passionate than was strictly necessary. George said nothing. He sat there doggedly, smoking my cigars and rubbing his rash, which the ointment had done little to help. His name was all over the newspapers. The *Daily Express* had called him the "Ceck monster." It had referred to the "abomination" of the "bones in the marsh" that had shocked this "sleepy village" in the "depths" of the countryside. The press assumed that George was responsible for the entire abomination, and was shrill in its clamor for his prompt capture. The village was crawling with reporters, and half-a-dozen of the creatures were even then clustered at the gates of Crook.

They'd already got to John Crowthorne, but he'd played the rustic bumpkin and claimed total ignorance, as he had to the police also, which left George, poor George, to bear the brunt alone. What was his *plan*, I asked him. What did he intend to *do*? I certainly hoped, I said, that he wouldn't draw *me* into it.

There was, at that moment, a knock at the door of the barn. George rose to his feet. I moved toward the door, turning to wave him into the shadows. The door swung open; framed against the light stood Fledge. For a moment nothing happened. I turned my eyes from Fledge and saw George disappearing beneath the dinosaur. Fledge had seen him, of this I have no doubt, for without delivering whatever message he'd come with he abruptly stepped out of the barn and the door swung shut behind him.

I lingered another moment in indecision. George had vanished into the obscurity. "Stay there!" I cried, then ran across the barn and through the door—which is low, and is set into one of two massive arched gates fastened with studded iron hinges. On impulse I locked it behind me. Fledge was moving rapidly toward the house. I caught up to him before he reached the porch, and clutched him by the arm. "Fledge," I gasped, "you saw nothing just now! Do you understand me? Nothing!" The man displayed not a twitch, not a flicker; but I saw it all the same, I saw the sudden flare of exultant power—the triumphalism—in him. He had me, and he knew it, this I could see in his long blank face, in those reddish eyebrows that lifted, perhaps, a millimeter, in scorn, I could see it in those thin and bloodless lips that may, I now think, have betrayed the merest tiny quiver of derision as he realized how dumbly I had played into his hands, how clumsily I had given him the game. And then the slight bow, the subtle gesture of contemptuous deference. "Very well, Sir Hugo," he said. My fingers were still gripping his arm. Glancing about me, I now saw Harriet standing at the drawing-room window, and gazing at us with intense perplexity.

Fledge returned to the house, and I to the barn. "George!" I shouted. "George!" But he had gone, out through the loose plank at the back that he had forced open three days previously.

Within fifteen minutes Limp was at Crook with four carloads of policemen. They poured into the barn and into the house, into the gardens and the orchard. I was in the drawing room with Harriet when, about half-an-hour after that, George emerged from the trees beside the driveway between several policemen. He had been handcuffed. Never before have I seen such black rage in a man's face. Just as they pushed him into the back of one of the cars he lifted his eyes to the face of Crook and spat on the gravel. Fledge was not at the window with us to observe this.

I AM, AS I say, in the kitchen as I remember all this, and I find myself attempting to postpone telling you what happened next. For we are drawing close to the cerebral accident that has condemned me to this wheelchair—this *hell*chair!—and reduced me to the status of a vegetable. Doris, having finished the washing up, comes and sits down opposite me, and pours us each a glass of wine. Dear Doris, I would much rather talk about her, quite frankly. She drinks much more heavily now than she ever used to, this I have had ample opportunity to observe, for in the past she never indulged herself to excess until her day's work was done. Now, though, Fledge seems to have relaxed his stern prohibition in this regard; he turns a blind eye when she miscalculates, as she usually does, and becomes incoherent by six. She doesn't have to conceal her drinking anymore, she told me during one of our "chats," and though this robs the activity of a good deal of its pleasure she has determined, she says, to take advantage of the new, permissive regime. With the result that when Fledge comes into the kitchen before dinner, he usually finds his wife standing rather unsteadily at the stove and clutching a pot of vegetables either crisped to black cinders or raw. "Shan't be long," she calls, hearing him enter and trying not to lurch; and he, quietly frowning, will take over, pull the meal together in some fashion, and serve it himself. Doris sinks into her chair by the stove and, no longer fit to knit, as was her habit in better days, tipples gently toward oblivion.

But these "chats" that we enjoy, Doris and I: they occur in the kitchen, usually in the evening but often earlier in the day, and they include the consumption, by Doris, of at least two bottles of sherry, bordeaux, or burgundy. No great connoisseur, Doris, but there are two things she likes in a wine, quantity and bite. And the cellars of Crook, amply stocked over several generations—we Coals like our bottle—offer her plenty of wine with plenty of bite. This is what happens: she pushes my wheelchair up to the table, and sets a glass before me. She fills my glass. Then, settling herself on the other side of the table, she fills her own glass. I sit there and gaze at her as she lifts it and gives me my health. She then proceeds deliberately and loquaciously to drink herself stupid. And throughout, she addresses all her "chat" to me, even going so far as to respond to the imaginary responses I have made to her inanities. And why, you ask, does Fledge permit her to do this? It's a question that intrigued me for some time. Then I realized: because he is upstairs, fornicating with Harriet in her bedroom in the west wing, and it suits them both very nicely to have Doris "out of commission." Fledge actually encourages her drinking, these days, for this very reason.

And so Doris drinks and chats, and I have come to know well the successive phases through which she passes on the road to oblivion. Doris is one of those in whom the first drink of the day can arouse a sense of consummate fulfillment unrivaled in the spectrum of human gratification. She is aware, too, that it is only in the satisfaction of an *illicit* desire that pleasure in its fullest measure can be known. So she fills her glass with wine, almost to the top, and there is, I can tell, in its sweet odor, and its ruby hue, a feast for the woman's sensorium, even before she tastes it. She lifts the brimming glass to her eager, parted lips and again pauses, prolonging for one delicious instant more the anticipation of drinking. There is no sound from the hall or staircase; the smell of the wine, slightly musky, is strong in her nostrils. She tips the glass. She swallows, in one long, ecstatic draft, half its contents and then, slumping in her chair with a deep sigh, picks up the bottle and gazes at it, taking a sort of supplementary pleasure in its shape and its label, the outward signs of the essence within. She finishes that first glass in two further movements, and sits a moment permitting the glow to mount from her belly to her brain. And then, as the familiar misty warmth begins to kindle, she will compliment me on my cellar.

I wonder, has it ever occurred to you that a certain analogy can be drawn between drinking and suicide?

It's very apparent to me, who can now partake of neither form of release and am, instead, literally incarcerated within my own flesh. But what the drinker would doubtless spurn is the *sudden* death, the *sudden* blessed cessation of experience, and liberation from the self, that the suicide craves. Sudden death is anathema to the drinker, for the approach to the void must be gradual, it must be attenuated. And so I observe Doris tantalizing herself, dallying over the first three-quarters of the first bottle, even, at times, consuming a slice of bread and a raw onion to further defer, to *cunctate* (lovely word, Latin *cunctari*, to linger) the delicious onset and progress of her drunkenness. "Steady now, Doris old girl," she murmurs, as she rises clumsily to her feet to drain and refill my glass—she drinks for both of us—and bumps against the table as she does so, spilling red wine onto the old scrubbed boards. The back door is still open, and the sounds and smells of the early evening come drifting in, birdsong, manure, the bark of a dog on a distant farm, and Doris, one ear cocked for Fledge coming down the passage, sits drinking with me, talking of the years in Kenya, then gazing off with filmed eyes into unseen stadiums of memory. What does she think of, I wonder at such times, though I know that her mind, by this stage, strictly speaking is not thinking but instead drifting in the vague, associative, oceanic way that the mind does when it sloshes off beyond language and surrenders to the booze. I am no stranger to it myself.

It grows dark outside, and the *putt-putt-putt* of a tractor comes from the road beyond the gates of Crook. Doris has opened her second bottle, and her oceanic consciousness is becoming befogged, benumbed, and her eyes have acquired a glazed fixity not unlike my own. Strands of silver hair come drifting loose from her bun, and though she is slumped untidily in the chair a certain mechanical precision is evident in her gestures, the lifting of the glass has come to resemble the operation of an automaton.

At last she rises from her chair and moves with slow, careful steps to the back door, which she closes and latches against the night. No lamp has yet been lit; moonlight spreads a weak and silvery glow across the kitchen, and beyond its cold fingers the shadows thicken, deepen, clot. Doris stiffly resumes her chair and gazes across the table at me. What must I look like now, I wonder—rigid and upright, with the moonlight gleaming from the great hook of my nose, my eyes in their hollows mere pinpricks of brightness in the gloom of the evening? A grotesque; a grotesque, locked in the grotto of his own bones. "Sir Hugo," murmurs Doris, "oh, Sir Hugo." She lays her head on her arms and begins to sob softly in the darkness, and I gaze on, unmoving, but not unmoved, across her quietly heaving shoulders and through the kitchen window to the moonlit yard beyond. It is then that I would wish to weep, too, but cannot—not because the ability to weep is blocked, as everything else is blocked, but because I'm much too old to learn to weep in the presence of another person. And this is another of those ironies, those inversions, of the vegetable state. It is long training, you see, that prevents me from weeping in public, with the result that the only means I have of communicating to the world that I am mentally alive and that I can *feel*—I cannot employ. I cannot employ it because the habit of self-restraint, maintained over a lifetime, is impossible to break. So, when not in the private darkness of my grotto, I preserve the dry-eyed, manly fortitude— of a fossil!

How vividly it all comes back to me, as I sit in the darkened kitchen and listen to Doris weeping herself to sleep. For as she weeps I remember the night—it was just after the first snow—that I compromised her, that I imposed my long-dormant sex instincts upon her; and I remember, too, the disgust I felt at the shabbiness, the vulgarity, and the intemperance of my behavior.

It happened during Harriet's Christmas party. She does this every year, throws a party for the local gentry; it's a thing we have to do, she says, one of the "proprieties." She extracts from me a promise to be welcoming and normal, and I invariably station myself by the Christmas tree and make sure the scotches keep coming at a steady clip. There was an awful lot of babble this year, and I'd managed to put up with Freddy Hough's so-called conversation for about ten minutes when it suddenly occurred to me to wonder where Cleo was (this was the day she'd come back from Oxford). I realized that I'd missed the girl, so I promptly abandoned Freddy and set off to the kitchen to find her. She was not there; but I did find Doris, loading a tray with cocktail sausages.

The kitchen was hot, Doris was working hard, and her face was damp with perspiration. Strands of hair clung wetly to her brow. She wore a freshly laundered black uniform with white cuffs, collar, and apron, and it fitted her narrow frame quite snugly. I sat down and, lighting a cigar, watched with some pleasure as she bustled between oven and table. "I bet you'd like a drink, Mrs. Fledge," I said. The noise of the party drifted down from the front of the house, muted and distant.

"I would dearly love a drink, Sir Hugo," she said, barely pausing in her work, "but there's the sausages to be seen to, and then I've to open more sardines."

"Let me help," I said. "I used to be an expert at opening sardines. In Africa," I added.

This time she stopped, and stood pushing the hair out of her eyes. "Oh no, Sir Hugo," she said. "I couldn't do that."

"Nonsense," I said. "I intend to abolish the division of labor; it's inherently unjust. Give me the sardines, Mrs. Fledge!"

Sardine tins, as you know, are opened with a sort of key with a slit in it, into which one inserts a small metal tongue that protrudes from the edge of the tin; by turning the key, one peels away the lid of the tin and reveals the oily treasures within. If you break off the little tongue, however, the task becomes much more complicated. I broke off the little tongue, and in the process cut my finger. "Damn!" I cried.

Doris came over with a worried frown. I was sitting at the table. She lifted my hand and peered at the tiny cut, from which had swelled a single drop of blood. She carried a faint odor of cocktail sausages, mingled with sweat. Like a fool I slipped my hand up the inside of her leg. I felt the roughness of her nylons. "No, Sir Hugo," she hissed, her eyes wide with horror as she backed away. I went after her—can you believe this of me?—I went after her. I knew that Fledge was certain to appear in the kitchen at any moment, and still I did it. "Sir Hugo!" hissed Doris, retreating rapidly across the kitchen towards the stove. Doubtless I presented a bizarre and frightening spectacle, wild-eyed from whisky, bleeding from the finger, and manifestly out of control. I trapped her in the corner. Doris is a head taller than me, and the kiss I attempted to plant on her mouth missed completely, my chin barely grazing her shoulder. But I did get a hand on one of her little breasts, so audaciously pointy in that tight black uniform. And then it happened, precisely what I'd known would happen—a loud, bogus cough from the doorway, and there stood Fledge, clutching an empty silver tray and glaring at me with what, for him, was fury. Doris scampered out of the corner and, sniffing once or twice, and with lowered eyes, set about loading the empty tray with sausages. I ran a hand through my hair; it was all smeared with blood, I noticed, as was Doris's apron. "Ha!" I said jauntily. Then: "Well!" Then, mustering my dignity, I sauntered across the kitchen, buttoning by dinner jacket and straightening my bow tie. "Excuse me," I said, eyeing the man, and cleared my throat rather noisily. For a moment Fledge did not move; then he stepped aside from the door, glancing sharply at my blood-smeared fingers, and I made my way back to the party.

My reaction, as I say, was one of profound self-disgust. At breakfast the next morning Harriet chattered brightly about who had and had not enjoyed themselves, about some old dowager who'd been sick into the gramophone, and why no one would touch the ham after that. "Still, the cocktail sausages were a great success, don't you think? You seemed to like them, Hugo."

I did not dignify this with a reply. In the cold light of sobriety I was squirming with shame, and quite unable to look Fledge in the eye, despite what I knew about *him*. I was simply not up to small talk about cocktail sausages. After breakfast I holed up in the barn. The one dim ray of hope was that the Horns were arriving in a few days. The house, I thought, would then be so full of bustle, the thing would have a chance to "blow over." Ha!

And even as I remember that night, Fledge himself silently enters the kitchen. Doris by this point is splayed slackly in her chair, her head thrown back and her mouth wide open, snoring loudly and stinking of wine. He stands there for a moment before rousing her, he gazes down at her long, white, scraggy neck, her stretched, inviting gullet, and I watch his face, see his lips twitch, as a certain familiar temptation returns; but he never succumbs, for he has his *plan*, you see; and it is my guess that Doris won't be removed from the picture until I myself am dead. We will never know if I am right or wrong, but had I a voice I would say to Doris: flee, woman, flee for your life!

He wakes her, and in due course she stumbles off to bed, and I sit there in my wheelchair, staring at the shadows on the ceiling and hoping for sleep. But in my mind's eye I see Fledge moving through the darkened house, locking doors and turning off lights, and then, with his candle, ascending the staircase and making his way past one window and then another into the west wing, to a bedroom where a light still burns. Ten or twelve minutes pass; all is still; out there in the countryside, the usual wealth of night sounds, a gust of wind moving suddenly through the trees, a fox barking at the moon. In Harriet's bedroom, only a candle burns now; the butler's clothes are neatly arranged upon a chair, beneath which gleam his shoes, their decorative perforations tiny points of blackness in the flickering gloom, and his socks neatly balled and tucked into the left one. The bedcovers are folded back and Fledge, naked, reclines on one elbow on the white sheet, and the candlelight touches his body with a shadowy glow. A line of fine, reddish-brown hair runs from the very center of his chest to his navel, and from there spreads lightly over his lower belly to be swallowed in the silky denseness of his pubic hair. A slight chubbiness is apparent about his chest and belly, a slight hint of fattening in a man who otherwise retains the leanness of his youth. He has long, well-formed legs covered with a fine red down that licks about his crossed ankles and reappears as mere filmy wisps on the arches of his shapely feet. At the fork of his body the penis lies slumbering on the testicular sac, the nicked dome of its dark head silvered by a stray moonbeam and the stem thickly and blackly corded with veins, while about it, like the wings of a sprite, spreads a fleece of soft red pubic hair. He is gazing through languid and half-closed eyes toward the window, where Harriet, *my* Harriet, stands in a billowing white nightgown, her hair loosed and tumbling, and pulls closed the curtains against the moon. She turns, and approaches the bed, thinking she comes to a man and failing to see that he is a monster.

YES, A MONSTER. What else are we to think him, that furtive, ruthless, doubly inverted creature? Harriet deserves all she gets at his hands, for she went in with her eyes open. Actually I don't believe he's interested in her at all. I believe he suffers from an acute sense of inferiority, and this manifests in pathological jealousy—of me. Hence his interest in Harriet. To be honest, I think he's clinically insane, a paranoid schizophrenic, in fact. But it's his treatment of Doris I'm concerned with now, it's his callous negligence and infidelity to that good woman that infuriate me beyond reason—though of course one would hardly expect better from a homosexual. Yes, Fledge is a homosexual, of the worst type, and if there remains any doubt in your mind on that score, then allow me to describe to you now the circumstances surrounding my cerebral accident.

We must return to the middle of February, to the days immediately following George's arrest. I had of course been questioned by the police, but no charges had yet been laid with regard to my harboring a fugitive from justice. Unable to tolerate the atmosphere in the house, I had been spending all my time in the barn, attempting to turn my mind to paleontology once more. I was in there one afternoon when, at about two thirty, there came a knock at the door. I can picture all too clearly, now, the strained and bulging blood vessel inside my skull, its leakage clotted on the thin inner wall which, even as the knocking died away, was rapidly losing the ability to bear the pressure of my thudding blood. "Come!" I shouted. It was Fledge.

He closed the door behind him and approached my chair. He carried a tray upon which was set my lunch, for I had not been into the house since breakfast. "Put it down there, Fledge," I said, gesturing vaguely at the small table. The man's presence aroused considerable antagonism in me, for it was only a few days since he had quite deliberately ignored my appeal regarding George. I have mentioned the aura of triumphalism he had seemed to emanate when I'd made that appeal, out on the driveway, the unspoken relish with which he'd grasped the fact that I had, as it were, given him the game: I felt that same vindictive exultation oozing from him now. But I had as yet formulated no satisfactory plan for "getting back" at him. You see, I could hardly rebuke him for having informed the police that a fugitive from justice was on the grounds of Crook, without revealing the extent of my own involvement in the affair. "That's all, Fledge," I said, not even turning in my chair.

He coughed lightly. "Your jacket, Sir Hugo," he said. I was still in the brown lab coat I wore while working.

"Oh yes," I said. I rose to my feet, and he helped me out of the lab coat. Laying it on the back of the chair, he then held open my tweed jacket, and I thrust my arms into the sleeves. He patted the shoulders once or twice, then brushed at the thing with the side of his palm. "Don't fuss, Fledge," I snapped. "That'll do."

"Very good, Sir Hugo," he murmured, and then, coming round, he moved the small table in front of my chair. "Wine, Sir Hugo?"

"Yes of course," I said, resuming my seat. He uncorked a bottle of burgundy and poured me a glass, and then stood by as I began to eat. "That's all right, Fledge," I said irritably, glancing up at the man as I chewed a potato. "You can go."

"Ah, Sir Hugo?" he said.

"What is it, Fledge?" I washed down the potato with a mouthful of burgundy.

"A young man from the village called at the house this morning; he wished to know if you would be requiring a new gardener."

"A new gardener? Christ almighty, are the vultures gathering already? Certainly not. I expect George Lecky to be back with us quite soon."

"Very good, Sir Hugo." Still he did not leave; he hovered by the table like a waiter.

"That's all, Fledge. You can go."

"Yes, Sir Hugo." He poured me more wine. He bent down and picked up a threepenny bit from under my chair, and put it on the table.

I laid my knife and fork down on my plate with a clatter. "Well good God man, what is it? What are you hanging about for? What do you want?"

"Sir Hugo, I wished only to say how sorry I am about everything that's happened."

I responded to this with an ironic snort. "That's hard to believe," I said. Then I glanced up at him. His expression had changed. The masklike blankness was touched now with a sort of subtle derision. Hard to say quite how I realized this; I could see it in the glint in his eyes, I think, in the flicker of mockery at the corners of his mouth.

"No, it's true, Sir Hugo," he said, in very soft, very silky tones—and then he reached out a hand, and *put it on my shoulder*!

I was out of my chair in an instant, and in the process I managed to knock over the table. Glass and china shattered on the floor as I shouted: "How dare you touch me!"

He backed off a little. He was watching me intently, his head slightly lowered and his hand to his lip, which he appeared to have bitten when I'd pushed him away, for there was blood on his mouth. I was furious; my fists were clenched, my eyes were flashing, I was seething like an angry little bantam. I had never been insulted in such a fashion—now he would have to go, no question! He took a step toward me. "Back off, you bastard!" I shouted. "No more of your foul tricks!"

He paid no attention. He advanced, menacingly, a

sneer now twisting his stained lips. The fumes of spilt wine were rising all about me and making my head spin. A very bad pain had begun to throb in my left temple. "Don't try it, Fledge," I warned him. My blood was in hot turmoil—there was going to be physical violence, this I now saw, and I was damned if I'd be bested by Fledge. His teeth suddenly gleamed in the light, and he grinned—and then he came at me, seized me by the hair with one hand and with the other gripped my wrist. Holding me thus he then dropped to one knee, and though I flailed and struggled like a wild thing he forced me down with him until I lay sprawled upon the floor, crablike and ungainly, with my head upon his arched thigh, and his fingers still knotted in my hair. In helpless rage I could do little but gaze up into his face; his expression had again changed, for now I read there only a sort of cold hunger, a cold light in his dead eyes and a cold and rather twitchy little smile on his pale thin lips, where there still remained a light smear of blood. A lick of his reddish hair had worked loose in the struggle and fell over his forehead in a floppy curve. I was powerless to resist as he brought his face down close to mine; and then his grinning features filled my vision entirely. I closed my eyes, the pain in my head now dreadfully intense. After a moment I felt it, and you may imagine my disgust: his mouth upon mine.

All the strength seemed to drain out of my body then. At last he lifted his face from this unholy kiss, and there was fire in his eyes, as he regarded me with a sort of brisk amusement; then suddenly I felt the grip of his fingers tighten in my hair, and he yanked my head violently backwards—and several things happened at once. I was now gazing straight up into the roof of the barn, where I saw the crow flap through the shadows from one rafter to another. At the same time there was a hot burst of searing pain in my head; and a sudden rapping at the door of the barn. "Daddy?" I heard Cleo calling from outside. "Daddy?"

Fledge quickly lifted his head from my throat and turned toward the door. His fingers slackened their grip in my hair, as he knelt there, alert and upright, concentrating on the voice from beyond the door. He seemed to forget me entirely; he let me go, and rose to his feet, allowing my body to slide like a rag doll off his thigh and onto the floor. And there I lay, as that weary, worn-out blood vessel in the inferior frontal convolution of my left hemisphere burst open; and as the blackness swept over me I was aware only of his footsteps receding toward the door, from behind which Cleo's voice could still be heard, saying: "Daddy?"

How long did I lie there? What happened at the door of the barn? It seems I will never know. But it's impossible not to speculate on what I might be now, if Fledge had raised the alarm immediately, if he had not simply left me there to die. Is it unreasonable, then, that I should take this obscure attempt on my own life as proving beyond a shadow of a doubt his guilt with regard to Sidney's?

CLEO IS COMFORTABLE in the kitchen. She can talk freely here, not oppressed, as she always is in the drawing room, by her conviction that Fledge is the evil creeping thing that murdered Sidney, and that Harriet is complicit with him. Doris is a nonthreatening figure, and I, Hugo, the girl has come to realize, am the perfect ally, for while I understand all she says, and she knows I understand it, I will never reprimand her, nor, worse still, show her the pitying sympathy that Harriet invariably displays toward her. With the result that she has gradually opened up to me, and as Doris goes about her duties, peeling potatoes and whistling tunelessly between sips of sherry, Cleo sits beside me at the kitchen table, smoking cigarettes and endlessly arranging her and my intermingled nail clippings in those elaborate circular designs, and chattering away about any odd thing that comes into her head as long as it doesn't touch upon Sidney or Harriet or Fledge. She was occupied thus the day Harriet came into the kitchen and said: "Mrs. Fledge, I'm going to have to ask you a favor. Mrs. Giblet is coming down to see me on Thursday, and Fledge won't be here. Could you stand in for him, I wonder?"

"Yes madam," said Doris, meekly.

"Oh good. Thank you so much. Cleo—"

Nothing. The girl was at the kitchen window, gazing into the yard. She did not turn round. Harriet was not within my line of vision, but I could all too easily imagine the moue of irritability and concern that this behavior provoked. "I do wish," said Harriet, "that you wouldn't drink in the afternoon, Mrs. Fledge. So bad for you"—and then she was gone. The point was, though, that the old woman would undoubtedly bring news of George. Two months had passed since his arrest, and I had heard nothing.

Fledge was away from Crook the day Mrs. Giblet came—the reason for his absence will become clear in due course—so it was Doris who announced the old woman's arrival. I was in the drawing room, gazing at the chimneypiece, and Harriet was sitting by the fire, reading a novel. It was rather a damp, cool afternoon, I seem to remember, and I had my tartan horse blanket tucked about my legs. Harriet sighed, and after carefully marking her place in the book with a dead matchstick, rose to her feet. In came Mrs. Giblet, in that huge fur coat of hers, and took both Harriet's hands in her own. "Dear Lady Coal," she wheezed, in husky tones, "such difficult times, for all of us."

"Indeed Mrs. Giblet," said Harriet. "Do sit down, won't you? Tea, please, Mrs. Fledge."

But Mrs. Giblet did not sit down. Instead, she turned toward me. Harriet, too, turned toward me, and the pair of them stood there, gazing at me, and I gazing back. The old woman was without her lapdog, but she did have her stick, and as she gazed at me she wrapped her claws about the handle and leaned on the thing. Her eyes bored into me like a pair of spiral drills, and as the seconds ticked by Harriet grew visibly uncomfortable. She laid a hand on her visitor's sleeve. "Do sit down, won't you, Mrs. Giblet?" she repeated.

"Poor fellow," said Mrs. Giblet, and began fumbling in the pockets of her coat for cigarettes; still she did not sit down. "Terrible thing, Lady Coal"—she turned toward Harriet—"how distressing for you. And him such a sprightly man, in his way."

"Life goes on, Mrs. Giblet," murmured Harriet. She found it distasteful, I know, to have to account for her feelings. I was now a source of embarrassment to her.

"And there's no hope, they say?" Mrs. Giblet's eyes were on me again. "His faculties will not return?"

"Apparently not, Mrs. Giblet."

"And he will live out his normal span, Lady Coal?"

Harriet winced at the brutal candor of this inquiry. "One doesn't know," she murmured. "One hopes and prays for the best, Mrs. Giblet."

"Whatever that may be. Tragic. And him still a young man."

"Hugo is over fifty," said Harriet quietly.

Mrs. Giblet snorted. "That's young, Lady Coal, believe me!" She had managed to get a cigarette into her mouth by this stage. There was the flare of a match and a cloud of blue smoke. "He can still smoke, I suppose?"

"Good heavens, Mrs. Giblet, it never occurred to me!" said Harriet and, apparently abandoning the effort to get the old woman to sit down, herself resumed her armchair. In point of fact I should have greatly enjoyed a cigar, but this was the first time anyone had thought of it. Mrs. Giblet did not pursue the point, unfortunately; she shuffled over to the armchair opposite Harriet's, and lowered herself stiffly into it. "Such a sad thing to lose a husband before his time," she said. "You're still a young woman yourself, Lady Coal. Not as young as I was—I lost Sidney's father when I was barely thirty, you know."

"No," said Harriet, "I didn't know. Ah, Mrs. Fledge." Doris appeared with the tea tray.

"Struck by a locomotive in Victoria Station. But that's by the by. Lady Coal, I spoke to the solicitors this morning. The news is not good, I'm afraid. Lecky refuses to plead insanity."

"Oh dear," said Harriet, who was not really equipped to deal with any of this.

"Oh dear indeed," said Mrs. Giblet. "We must think very hard what's best, Lady Coal. I'm afraid if he sticks to his story he'll swing."

Swing!

"But I believe it's the truth, Mrs. Giblet! George Lecky simply doesn't have that sort of violence in him."

"Oh, I agree," said Mrs. Giblet. "But if I under-

stand Sir Fleckley correctly"—she referred to Sir
Fleckley Tome, a barrister—"he will not be believed.
This business has aroused strong emotion in the popular
breast, Lady Coal; even a partial admission of guilt, he
says, will tip the scales."

"But George must tell the truth," said Harriet.
"Surely that's enough? This *is* England, after all."

Her faith was touching.

"Dear Lady Coal," said Mrs. Giblet, "your faith is
touching. But you see, it will be assumed that a man
who could stumble upon a dead body and feed it to his
pigs is a man who could kill. We tend to lose the fine
distinctions when it comes to such things." It was hard
to believe she was talking about her own son.

"Yes, I do see, Mrs. Giblet. All the same—"

"Public opinion is already strongly against him, Lady
Coal. Have you been reading the papers?"

"Oh, Mrs. Giblet, I haven't. I find it all too distressing. To think that George Lecky—no, it doesn't bear
contemplating. But this is *frightful*, Mrs. Giblet! You
mean that if George tells the truth he'll be hanged, and
if he lies he won't?"

"Yes," said Mrs. Giblet.

There was a silence. "Then what is to be done?"
said Harriet.

"That," said Mrs. Giblet, "is precisely what I came
to Crook to talk to you about. My interest in the case
is very simple, Lady Coal; perhaps it's unnecessary for
me to say this, but like you, I don't believe George
Lecky killed my son. But if he swings—"

"Please, Mrs. Giblet," said Harriet; the word clearly
distressed her.

"If he is found guilty, Lady Coal, then Sidney's murderer will go free. This I most emphatically do not wish to happen."

"No," said Harriet, "of course not."

"Lady Coal," said Mrs. Giblet, "let me ask you frankly: who killed Sidney?"

"Oh, Mrs. Giblet, if I knew—"

"Tell me your suspicions, Lady Coal, no matter how bizarre they seem."

"Well, I don't know, I hardly think—"

"Has it ever occurred to you, Lady Coal, that your husband was in any way involved?"

"Rubbish!" The door flew open, and there stood Cleo—she had been listening in the hallway! Into the room she darted, her eyes flashing, and over to the fireplace, where she stood with her back to the fire between the two seated women, who, clasping their teacups, gazed at her in wide-mouthed astonishment. "Rubbish!" she hissed, all coiled up in her baggy black cardigan like a scorpion. "You foul old woman," she cried, her voice charged with scorn and rage, "you ghastly old hag, you come floundering in here like a stinking whale and start accusing my father! How dare you! What gives you the right? You get out of here, with your foul lies! Get out, you hear!"

"My dear girl—" said Mrs. Giblet, stiffening with anger.

"*Cleo!*" breathed Harriet.

Cleo's voice grew wild. "You sat on Sidney all his life," she shouted. "You mocked him and terrorized him, you tried to turn him into your slave! It's a wonder there was anything left of him at all, after growing up with you!''

"Sidney was a weak boy," said Mrs. Giblet, with some contempt. "He needed a firm hand."

"A firm hand!" cried Cleo. "You call what you did to him a firm hand?"

"Perhaps," snapped the old woman, "a firm hand would have done you some good, young lady."

"You bloody old witch!" screamed Cleo, and flailed at her in that clumsy way that women have when they try to punch each other, all stiff-armed swings. Harriet screamed and leaped to her feet, and as she tried to pull Cleo away from the old woman a teacup fell off the table and smashed to pieces on the floor. For several moments there was a chaos of flailing arms and wild shrieks until at last there came a resounding *smack!* and Cleo stepped back, stunned, toward the fireplace, one hand to her cheek, and Harriet, aroused as I'd rarely seen her before, stood glaring at the girl in a positively Churchillian posture, and old Mrs. Giblet, with one gnarled claw upon her massive heaving bosom, and the other nervously touching her hair and face, as though to assure herself that no appendage had been torn off in the fracas, attempted to regain her composure.

"Apologize, please, Cleo," said Harriet, breathing heavily. Cleo, her anger suddenly dissipated, dropped her head in that mutely defiant manner she had recently adopted. Harriet advanced upon her. "Apologize," she repeated, and there was a new tone in her voice, a tone of quietly dangerous authority. Cleo tried to brush past her, but Harriet was having none of it. She gripped the girl by the wrists and told her, for the third time, to apologize. "You're hurting me, Mummy," wailed Cleo, not at all the plucky girl she'd once been. But Harriet's dander was up, and she did not let go until at last Cleo turned to the old woman and mumbled: "I'm sorry, Mrs. Giblet."

The old woman had by this time regained her composure somewhat. She reared in her armchair, claws once more wrapped about her stick, head lifted, wattles awobble, and shot a glance of sheer majestic outrage at the defeated girl. "You will never, ever lay a finger on me again, young woman," she declared. "Is that clear?"

"Yes," mumbled Cleo.

"I beg your pardon?"

"Yes," said Cleo.

"Very well then," said Mrs. Giblet, settling herself. "I accept your apology."

"Sit down please, Cleo," said Harriet firmly, "and we shall have tea. Mrs. Fledge?" How long, I wondered, had Doris been in the room? Had she witnessed the entire squalid incident? "Mrs. Fledge, clear these things away, please, and bring us fresh tea. Now, Mrs. Giblet, where were we?"

But the old hag wasn't going to risk slandering me any further, that was clear. "I have requested permission to visit George Lecky in prison," she said, "and I am seeing my M.P. next week. I wonder if there's anything else that occurs to you, Lady Coal?"

But there wasn't.

When Mrs. Giblet had left—she'd taken a room at the Hodge and Purlet again, and would not be persuaded to stay at Crook, hardly surprising, really, after being attacked by Cleo—when she'd left, Harriet came back to the drawing room and sat down opposite Cleo. "Darling," she said, very seriously, "that was dreadful. It was outrageous. I don't think I've ever been so embarrassed. Whatever came over you?"

Cleo had resumed her drawing-room manner—the sunken head, the sulky silence. "Cleo!" said Harriet sharply. "Answer me!"

Then up came the girl's head, and fire flashed from her wild and tear-streaked eyes. "Didn't you *hear* her, Mummy? Didn't you hear what she said about Daddy?"

"Of course I did, darling," said Harriet, in slightly softer tones. "But she's only trying to help, you must understand that."

"Help? Calling Daddy a murderer? That's help?"

"She didn't call Daddy a murderer. Oh, I know, darling"—slowly the power was seeping out of her; Harriet was only truly potent when the proprieties were being flouted—"I do understand your point of view, but nothing justifies behavior like that, nothing."

"Mummy, how can you *say* that? She said Daddy was involved in Sidney's murder, and you sit by and do nothing, and all the time Daddy's sitting here, listening, and unable to defend himself."

"Daddy doesn't know what's going on, darling," said Harriet quietly. "And I'm sure Mrs. Giblet didn't mean to suggest that he had anything to do with what happened to Sidney."

"Of course she did! That's precisely what she meant! And anyway, Daddy does know what's going on. He understands everything."

"Cleo, dear"—a sharp note, here—"the doctors were quite clear about this. Hugo is not aware of what is happening around him."

"But he is, I tell you!"

"Darling, he's *not*. We've had the best neurologists in the country do extensive testing, and they're absolutely certain about this: Hugo is massively brain-damaged; he has no real consciousness of the world. He cannot *think*."

"He *can*."

"Cleo, you're making me angry. Do you suppose it was easy for me to accept? Do you think I didn't hold out every hope? Darling, I hate to have to tell you all over again, but these are the facts—Daddy's not able to think."

"He is."

"You're being silly, Cleo. You're imagining things. Why do you say this?"

"I just know."

"But *how*, darling?"

"I can tell by his eyes."

"Oh dear." Harriet sighed.

"And sometimes he cries."

"I daresay he does, darling, but crying doesn't mean anything. Daddy cried in hospital; it's an autonomous reaction, the doctors said—it's a cleansing process."

"I don't care. I know he knows everything that's happening."

"I don't wish to discuss this with you any further. These are fantasies, darling. I know you love Daddy, but you must accept what's happened. I've had to, and

God knows it's not been easy for me, either. Now would you please go and help Mrs. Fledge in the kitchen.''

Cleo slowly got to her feet and left the room, casting one long, warm glance in my direction. ''See you later, Daddy,'' she said. When the door had closed behind her Harriet sighed deeply and did something she did very rarely: she took a cigarette from the box on the mantelpiece and smoked it by the window, gazing out at the pond in front of the house. From time to time I could feel her looking over at me in a faintly quizzical manner; then, after tossing the butt in the fireplace, she left the room, and I was alone. But her words seemed to echo in my skull, and as I sat there staring at the chimneypiece, at the coat-of-arms and the motto, I could hear her insisting, on best authority, that I was unable to think. If I couldn't think, what then is all this? A figment of Cleo's imagination?

THE NEXT MORNING there came another shock. I had not as yet had an opportunity to assimilate the events of the afternoon—and there was much to assimilate, with regard not only to George, but also to myself. For though there was no logical reason why Harriet's insistence upon my inability to think should disturb me—it's self-evident, after all, that I can—yet all the same I was shaken by it, shaken to the core. As though my identity were merely a reflection, or construct, of the opinion of others. I found myself reeling, very much on the defensive, forced to assert my own self *to* myself and thus confirm that I was, still, in effect, viable. Can you understand that? It was, then, in this very shaky state, this state of ontological instability, so to speak, that I was forced to cope with the implications of both Mrs. Giblet's visit *and* an attempted metamorphosis on the part of Fledge.

Yes, a metamorphosis. For, apparently with Harriet's consent (perhaps, it now occurs to me, at her instigation?) he had relinquished his morning suit, traditional uniform of the butler, and adopted, instead, a tweed jacket and twill trousers. He had gone up to London *in propria persona*, a butler, and returned disguised as a gentleman. I'm afraid I got these two events—the Giblet visit and Fledge's new clothes—rather muddled, and lost track of causation, agency, and empirical precision.

Probably I should begin by describing in closer detail what the man looked like when I saw him in the kitchen that morning. The jacket was, as I say, tweed, and not unlike my own. That is, it was slightly hairy, greenish-brown in color, with a fine herringbone pattern, leather patches on the elbows, and leather edgings on the cuffs. With wide lapels and square shoulders, it tapered to the waist then flared over the hips, and had two vents at the back. The buttons were leather-covered, and there were flaps on the pockets. The trousers were of a beige cavalry twill, sharply creased and with turnups that broke nicely on the insteps of a pair of highly polished, squeaky brown brogues. A well-tailored sports shirt with a quiet check, and a dark brown tie with a narrow yellow diagonal stripe; and thus Fledge, sleek and elegant, as he entered the kitchen for Harriet's breakfast tray. He was, as I say, pretending to be a gentleman; and it took a gentleman's nose, like mine, to detect the imposture.

I mentioned earlier that Fledge had an indefinable quality to him, a facet, I suggested, of his guarded and secretive nature. I said that he could be "anything," and that only the presence of Doris at his side served to situate and define the man. I was wrong. Watching him organizing Harriet's breakfast tray I realized that Fledge was no chameleon, a change of costume did not transform him, as he so clearly intended it to, into a gentleman. Something essential was lacking, a certain facial creasing, I think, that would denote affable skepticism and the expectation of deference—for such things show in a gentleman's face. Fledge looked like a steward, or a bailiff, one who almost straddles the chasm, but not quite. An interstitial man. An in-between man. He did not look ridiculous, but he did look indeterminate, as though he did not know his place.

Pondering the new Fledge I constructed a hypothesis. I imagined how, as he dressed himself each morning, in Harriet's bedroom, in the gloom of dawn, he must have resented assuming the garb of servility that the morning suit represented. For in Harriet's bed (from which he would have just arisen) a place of grace was available to him; in Harriet's bed he was an essential sexual man, whereas the moment he donned that morning suit he became once more the servant; this, clearly, was what lay behind the sudden, drastic transformation. Transformation I say; to me, then, it was experienced as a transgression, as a gross disturbance in the order of things, and this sense of disorder somehow fed into the turmoil I was experiencing as a result of Mrs. Giblet's visit, and intensified to the point of volcanic snorting my rage that George's dire predicament, my own increasingly wobbly grasp of things—the entire constellation of disturbances, in short—had their source and origin in the silent, ruthless, and violent ambition of this vulpine intruder. I was convulsed with mute fury and had to have my back thumped hard.

It rained all day—we had much rain at around this time—and the atmosphere in the kitchen was dark and subdued. Nobody mentioned Fledge's new clothes. Cleo looked awful; she had great black rings around her eyes, and I was sure she had not slept at all. Poor child, her coming so spiritedly to my defense, and then what she had suffered at the hands of the two older women—all this had clearly sapped her strength. I can't begin to say how touched I was that she would stand up for me so staunchly, my brave little elf; like George she had a core of integrity that was unshakeable and incorruptible; like him she maintained toward me a fierce protective loyalty now that I could no longer fight my own battles. After lunch, when Doris had finished washing the dishes and gone upstairs to "do out" Harriet's bedroom, the girl sat beside me at the kitchen table and began to speak. It was not immediately clear to me what, or rather who, she was talking about; she spoke of his being "very angry" with her; and though she did not use his name, I realized after a moment or two that she was referring to Sidney. I then understood *why* she thought he was angry with her—it was because she *had* used his name yesterday. This, apparently, was forbidden.

Poor, dear, haunted Cleo. She was so desperately alone, and I could only sit there, staring straight ahead, stiff as a plank of wood, and grinning. The rain came drizzling down into the back yard, drizzling down from a leaden sky in which the clouds hung oppressively low and heavy. She sat beside me, smoking cigarette after cigarette, and the tears rolled down her face as she mumbled on about Sidney, who was no longer, it seems, the pale and faintly sweet-smelling ghoulish creature she had conjured in a fit of hysterical weeping that night in February. His features were unrecognizable now, she said, owing to the copious discharge of a yellowy, viscous substance that oozed from his flesh. His eyes and ears and mouth were crawling with worms, she said. These were appalling nightmares for the child to experience, and I grew very angry with Harriet, that in her infatuation with Fledge she could permit her daughter to suffer like this, and I'm afraid I began to snort yet again. This at least served to rouse Cleo from her morbid and incoherent mumblings; she had to get up and pound me on the back, as she'd seen Doris doing on more than one occasion, until I could breathe properly once more.

A little later Doris herself came back downstairs and began to prepare tea, and Cleo relapsed into silence. When Fledge came in for the tray I noticed that three cups and saucers, and three plates, had been set out upon it. Were we to have visitors again? Was old Giblet coming back for more? As he picked up the tray, Fledge murmured to his wife that I was to be brought down to the drawing room. Cleo rose wearily from the kitchen table—she had been sitting there since after lunch—and followed him down the hallway. I came rumbling along in the rear, pushed by Doris, and in the gloom of that damp and miserable afternoon I could see, up front, the steam that issued from the spout of the teapot as it drifted up to the ceiling in little wispy puffs. There was a fire burning in the drawing room, and I was placed in my usual position, against the wall directly opposite. Cleo sank into her usual armchair, and Harriet sat at the tea table, as she always did, and poured. I was still puzzled as to who would get the third cup. I was not kept in suspense for very long; after Cleo had been given hers, Fledge took a cup and, having stirred in two spoons of sugar, *sat down* opposite Harriet and began to make conversation to her in low, inaudible tones. Cleo took in this development with barely a glance; for me, however, it demonstrated with shocking clarity just how absurd the entire situation was becoming. What sort of a house was this, that a homicidal butler who no longer wore his morning suit should sit down and drink tea with the mistress?

The weather continued miserably damp. Though I saw the man every day, I could not accustom myself to Fledge's new clothes, nor to his new role in Crook, which I found impossible to define. In some respects he still behaved as a servant, in others as some sort of a house guest. And though I no longer ate in the dining room, I came to suspect that he now occupied my chair at the head of the table during lunch and dinner.

Harriet was clearly happy with the new arrangements. In the evening she would drink a glass of brandy with him in the drawing room, and offer him one of my cigars. She herself was smoking several cigarettes a day at this time. I can see it now so clearly, and what a cloying little drama they always made of it. Harriet would take a cigarette from the proffered box, then sit forward on the edge of her armchair, frowning, the cigarette between her slightly trembling fingers, as the tall sleek man in the herringbone tweed jacket bent stiffly forward from the waist with his thumb deflecting the cap of the lighter; a slender flame sprang up like a tiny golden spearhead, and Harriet's eyes would flicker upwards to his. (The pair of them are framed against the fireplace for this touching little tableau.) She prolongs the operation for an instant longer than is strictly necessary; then, inexpertly expelling a lungful of smoke, she murmurs: "Thank you, Fledge," and sits back in her armchair, picking up her brandy glass and swirling its contents about in a manner entirely unfamiliar to me.

Did I mention how dearly I should have liked to go out to the barn and commune for a while with *Phlegmosaurus*? I missed the old scoundrel, frankly, and often wondered how he was. Well, one afternoon during this period Cleo apparently read my mind, for quite spontaneously she suggested to Doris that they do that very thing—that is, that the pair of them take me out to the barn. "Just for a little outing," said Cleo. "I'm sure he misses his bones, aren't you, Mrs. Fledge?"

It was raining again. Harriet had driven into Ceck, and Fledge was off somewhere by himself, probably in his pantry. There was thus nobody present to prohibit the expedition. Cleo procured raincoats and umbrellas, while Doris tucked me up warmly in the wheelchair. Fortunately there was a key to the barn hanging on a nail in the back kitchen.

We went out through the back door and across the yard to the gate that gave onto the driveway. Doris was pushing the wheelchair and Cleo was holding the umbrella. We bumped and scrunched across the gravel, in the rain, and Cleo kept up a cheery stream of chatter. It was months since I had seen the barn, and gazing at it now, as Cleo fiddled with the padlock, I felt a tremor of anxiety as to what I would find within. The door swung open, the wheelchair lurched over the threshold, and for the moment or two that Cleo hunted for the switch I beheld the familiar looming form, and felt the familiar surge of pride and awe, despite the stink of rotten hay and damp sacking that choked the barn. But then the lights flickered to life overhead, and I was able to see the toll the elements had taken in my absence. It was as I had feared; my dinosaur was overrun with fungus.

Damp was the problem. Nobody had thought to cover the bones, and the rain had been dripping through the roof for weeks. Everywhere the greenish mold endemic to this part of the county was in evidence. It clustered in spongy masses in the hollows of the bones, and licked outward in thin, blotchy fingers, and dripped from the jaws, and the long-clawed fingers, and the pelvis of the beast, in delicate lacy clumps. I was shocked at how quickly and how extensively *Phlegmosaurus* had been infested, and it was not difficult to imagine what a few more months of dampness and darkness would do to him: transform him into a huge living hulk of mold, the bones within merely the frame or scaffold of a voracious fungus. It depressed me acutely to observe all this, and I sat there in a state of bitter mortification as Cleo, apparently fascinated, wandered around the thing.

I was happy when Doris suggested we go back to the house lest I catch cold.

I presume it was the sight of *Phlegmosaurus* overgrown with fungus that provoked the dream I had that night, in which I discovered to my horror that my wheelchair was an excrescence of the living boards of Crook, and that I was its sentient blossom, that I was *growing into* my wheelchair, merging with it and in the process turning into a sort of giant plant. Hindered though I was from investigating my own extremities I *knew* somehow that green, leafy extrusions were sprouting from my back and my arse and my arms and legs and feet, and these extrusions, these sprouts and tendrils, had fused with the wood and the basketwork of the wheelchair, and had begun to crawl across the floorboards and clutch at table legs and doorknobs and electrical wires, and I knew they would in time colonize the entire structure, and bring it down; I would then merge organically with Crook and we would rot together on that high hill overlooking the valley of the Fling. God alone knows what monstrosity would sprout from our composting remains.

BREAKDOWN AND DECAY were much
on my mind, during those rainy days of late April. It
occurs to me, in retrospect, that perhaps I was merely
finding echoes in the outside world for that which I
intuitively understood to be happening within my own
body. Perhaps there's a limit, a threshold, to what a
man can take when his relation to the world is one of
pure passivity. Perhaps the world begins slowly to over-
whelm him, if he is without the power to react to it. Is
this feasible? I've told you about Harriet's assault, her
insistence on my inability to think, and how it weakened me. Inasmuch as George, and Cleo, and Doris,
and *Phlegmosaurus* were all dear to me, their respec-
tive breakdowns also weakened me, for I was acutely
conscious of my inability to intervene in any way—
watching things fall apart takes its toll, I discovered;

one tends to fall apart oneself. When, a few days later, George's trial began, I was not even equipped to provide him, at a distance, with the spiritual support he so desperately needed. I seemed able to muster only a sort of helpless, hopeless resignation as I saw how things would go with him. (Even in the kitchen of Crook the case was discussed, and in this way I was able to keep abreast of developments.) I did at least retain my imaginative faculties, and attempted to generate some idea of what the poor man was going through; whether it did him, or me, any good that I did this, I very much doubt.

Yes, it was of George that I was mostly thinking, as we emerged from that dismal rainy period and into springtime proper. I was imprisoned myself, locked away in a cage of bones, and so my sympathy for George in his prison of bricks and steel was rendered all the more poignant. That silent good man had been a sort of right arm to me ever since our first encounter in a sweltering and fetid little fly-infested, tin-roofed bar on the east coast of Africa, and for this reason I was now, despite my catalepsy, profoundly implicated in whatever fate should befall him.

I saw him in the dock. He stood between a pair of grim-faced, black-clad prison warders, meshing his eyebrows in fierce concentration as he gathered his depleted moral resources for the coming ordeal. Below him, in the well of the court, eminent counsel in tight-curled wigs of an unnatural whiteness murmured one to another, while over to his left was the witness stand, and beyond it the jury. Directly opposite him, and similarly elevated, sat the judge, Mr. Justice Congreve, an old man, and in my mind's eye I saw him survey his courtroom from bleary, tired eyes, as his bony fingers clutched the gavel then thumped it three times for order. When his moment came George stepped up to the rail of the dock and barked out in a deep, gruff, defiant voice: "Not guilty." He did not make a good impression at all. Mr. Justice Congreve had seen enough men in the dock to know at a glance that this one was going to swing.

Why do I say that? Why, even then, was I so certain that George was doomed? Perhaps because I was doomed myself, and could not help yoking his fate to mine. Bear with me, please, but those occasions when I was able to observe the events occurring around me with any vestige of objectivity were growing increasingly rare. In fact, I began to find that the only events that I *could* record with any real precision were not those that happened outside myself but, rather, the operations that my own mind performed upon the fragmentary stimuli that now constituted reality for me. And one of the most pernicious of these operations was the tendency to, as it were, cast nets of my own thought outward onto those close to me, and see them not as separate and distinct from myself but rather as extensions or manifestations of elements of my own mind. George, in other words, was becoming a bit of *me*, inasmuch as I was now able only to imagine his experience, and had only the most fragmentary means of testing my projections against reality. The same was true of Cleo and Doris, to a lesser extent. Oddly enough, the only ones I could see at all clearly were Harriet and Fledge.

Forgive me if I'm being tendentious. I do feel,

though, that in the interests of candor I should warn you of the distortions to which the passive and isolated mind is prone; you will perhaps take this into account, should I slip unwittingly into anomalous or contradictory positions. George was in the witness box—and this I am not inventing, but paraphrasing from the *Daily Express*—standing stiff as a ramrod, his hands gripping the rail so fiercely that the knuckles whitened to livid bony knobs. He had been called as first witness for the defense; Sir Fleckley Tome, prevented by the accused man from making a plea of insanity, was forced to argue that all the evidence was circumstantial. The entire courtroom listened attentively as he gently and carefully drew out George's version of *what happened* out on the Ceck Marsh that night, and so mellifluous, so utterly reasonable was the flow of the discourse Sir Fleckley produced that one could begin to feel the jury succumb, and this I imagine is an exhilarating feeling for a trial lawyer, though Sir Fleckley was, of course, far too experienced to express pleasure in his own rhetoric. So it was, then, that George, in the collective gaze of that packed courtroom, was gradually transformed from a monster in human form to a simple, decent man of the soil, a man who'd made a foolish blunder in failing to report the finding of Sidney's body—but a foolish blunder, Sir Fleckley implied, was by no means the same thing as capital murder. George Lecky was a foolish man, a wrong-headed man, but he was not a killer. And then he sat down.

As I say, I'm translating this from that appalling species of ''prose'' that organs like the *Daily Express* perpetrate upon their gullible and vulgar public. In any event, the apprehension I mentioned earlier (whatever its origins) that George was bound to swing, was to some extent dissipated by the account Cleo read me of that first morning's session. The afternoon, however, utterly dashed those hopes. For counsel for the prosecution, an energetic barrister called Humphrey Stoker cross-examined George so vigorously that he totally destroyed any faint aureole of innocence that might have begun to shimmer about him. Why, he wanted to know, had George failed to report finding a body out on the marsh? With withering scorn he lacerated George's somewhat inarticulate explanation, held it up to ridicule, implied that George was a liar, and then set about exploiting the pig-related aspect of the affair; and soon poor George was bathed once more in a lurid and terrible glow. Time and again a thrill of horror rippled around the courtroom as Mr. Stoker enlarged upon the events of that night—several women turned pale and had to leave the courtroom—and though Sir Fleckley repeatedly rose to his feet with objections to his learned friend's questions, Mr. Justice Congreve consistently overruled him. George grew increasingly tense, and his warders sensed it. "Take it easy, George," they murmured, but this was not a situation that George could take easily, not at all.

"I suggest to you," cried Mr. Stoker, who had worked himself into a fine lather of indignation, "that from some primitive motive hard for civilized men and women to understand, you plotted the killing of an innocent young man, and then you carried out your inhuman plan, and then you cold-bloodedly disposed of his body in the manner you yourself have described!"

"It's not true, damn you!" shouted George, incapable of further restraint. He leaned over the rail, banging his fist on the paneling of the box. "I didn't kill him, I tell you!"

Down came Mr. Justice Congreve's gavel. "Order!" cried the old man as a hubbub of excited chatter broke from the public gallery and drowned out George's shouts. "Order!" And then, at a nod from on high, the two warders clamped George's arms to his side and hauled him, still shouting, out of the courtroom and down to a cell below. Mr. Stoker, who had of course set out to provoke just such an outburst, wiped his brow with a snowy handkerchief and then sat down, glancing, as he did so, with one uplifted eyebrow, at Sir Fleckley; and Sir Fleckley made a wry moue at his colleague. The story appeared under the banner headline: CECK MONSTER DRAGGED FROM COURT: BLACK LECKY LOSES CONTROL.

But if that was bad, there was worse to come. For when, the next morning, Humphrey Stoker got George back on the stand, he elicited from him the shocking information that after feeding Sidney to the pigs, he'd then slaughtered those same pigs, butchered them, and *sent the meat to Crook!*

Cleo began to giggle hysterically, and Doris turned white; and I quickly realized that *all autumn and winter* we had been eating meat from Ceck's Bottom. And it was not only the Coals who were implicated. The local gentry had hungrily devoured sausages and ham sandwiches during Harriet's Christmas party. Patrick Pin and the Catholics had been in Crook on Christmas morning, drinking my sherry and eating ham sandwiches. The Horns had eaten ham with us on New Year's Eve, *and so had Mrs. Giblet*. We had all, indirectly, and unknowingly, eaten Sidney.

And then I thought of the satyrs of Ceck, sitting in George's kitchen on Christmas night with their bottles of brown ale and their roast haunch of pork; and it suddenly occurred to me to wonder, as I remembered their gusts of coarse rustic mirth, if they, unlike the rest of us, had *known*. It's a question that perplexes me still; but I rather think so.

I HAVE BEEN experiencing painful twinges from the region of my ticker. I have sclerotic coronary arteries, did I mention that? A bad heart; a faulty pump. Also, certain of my facial muscles have been pulled back and clamped tight in a rather ghastly grimace, a fierce, involuntary grin that never leaves my features now, regardless of what I am feeling. Often in the alcove I weep and grin simultaneously. My breathing is stertorous all the time, so I'm an unpleasant piece of work, all told, and I'm not surprised that Fledge turned my wheelchair to the wall that day, though of course there was a great deal more to the man's action than that.

But the rainy days of March and April were behind us now, and the weather was warm enough that I could be put out in the back yard for hours at a time. There I would sit, listening to the birds sing (those little di-

nosaurs!), and grinning at the gate in the old brick wall
on the far side. At other times I sat on the terrace just
outside the French windows and bestowed my smiling
bounty on the little jungle that the flower garden had
become. I saw George down there once, by the pond.
That day the garden was a riot of color, and so was I.
A garland of oak leaves encircled my skull, and peeping
through it was a pair of little white horns with blunt
tips. My forehead had fallen, my eyes slanted upwards,
and my brows came sweeping together at the root of
my nose like a pair of hairy handlebars. My mouth was
frozen in a broad, lascivious grin. George was on his
knees among the flowers, and when he saw me he rose
to his feet and stood with a weeding trowel in one hand
and the other shading his eyes from the sun, which
blazed down upon him from a cloudless blue sky and
reminded me of the days he'd gazed up the hill in Africa
at me, before setting off for the coast. The sun was
strong, and he seemed to shimmer, just as his reflection
in the black pond water would shimmer when a goldfish
rose to the surface for a bot-fly. He was wearing his
collarless blue policeman's shirt and his old brown cor-
duroys, but not his boots, I noticed, because his feet
were cloven now, he was a hoofed man, and a fringe
of coarse hair licked in thick bristly hanks over his goat-
ish ankles. Phantom, of course, projection of a crumbling mind; also I was bareheaded, exposed to the sun,
for Doris had forgotten my hat.

Another time I saw Fledge in the garden, and I saw
him die. He was lying naked in the grass. I've told you
what Fledge looks like naked: he is long and thin with
a very slight plumping of the flesh on his chest and

belly. He is very white, and a narrow line of reddish hair runs down his body from a point midway between those plump chests of his, all the way to his pubic hair. Cleo, all in black, was crawling toward him through the grass. She had a knife between her teeth. The sun was directly overhead, and shining so brilliantly that the blade was like a bar of molten silver. Cleo reared up on her knees and drove the shining knife into Fledge's heart. His body arched up as a great glob of blood and other body fluids exploded from his mouth. For a few moments his arched body shuddered in convulsion over the grass, and his mouth fell open; his eyes stared up at the sun. Then he subsided onto the earth with a long gasp. Another time, just as Cleo lifted the knife, he suddenly sat up and seized her wrists, and the pair of them began to struggle violently on their knees, then keeled over and writhed together in the grass. Events like these, if I can call them events, disturbed me greatly, for while I knew they were entirely illusory, at the same time they appeared quite real; they *felt* real. But they were hallucinations, merely, symptomatic of the sort of slippage, or dislocation, to which my mind was increasingly subject in the late spring.

But it was mostly George I saw down there. I would sit at the French windows and watch the fine spring rain come drifting like gauze upon the flower garden, where the untended weeds were crowding the blooms of the bulbs he'd planted in the autumn. The shrubs and the hedges spilled in an unruly manner onto the paths and flower beds, and their greenness had a peculiarly vivid quality to it, in that misty rain, a sort of viridescent effulgence that struck me as oddly and wildly beautiful.

The smell of the garden rose to my nostrils, the damp, rich smell of vegetation luxuriating in its own unchecked profusion, and as I gazed out over this hazy jungle, over the lily pond, which was spotted and circled with the gentle, unceasing rain, I grinned at the phantom of my imprisoned comrade toiling in the earth.

His trial only lasted five days, and Harriet stayed in London throughout, for she was to be called as a witness for the defense, a character witness. That's how weak George's case was: there was only the circumstantiality argument, and the testimony of Lady Coal. And even that backfired, for after Sir Fleckley had elicited from Harriet the opinion that George was trustworthy, decent, and incapable of violence, Humphrey Stoker rose to his feet and, examining his fingernails in an offhand manner, casually asked Harriet what precisely was the nature of her relationship with the accused man.

"He is my gardener," said Harriet.

"And what does this entail, Lady Coal?" said Stoker, removing his spectacles and absently polishing them on the hem of his robe.

"Well, the usual things," said Harriet. "I tell him what we need in the way of flowers and vegetables and so on, and he lets me know if, oh, if we must have a new wheelbarrow or whatever. Things to do with the garden."

"I see," said Stoker, and his voice was now dripping irony. "This is the nature of your relationship with the accused, Lady Coal: he lets you know if you must have a new wheelbarrow."

"Objection," said Sir Fleckley, wearily, rising to his feet.

"Overruled," said Mr. Justice Congreve.

"No more questions, my lord," said Stoker, and sat down.

Harriet looked for a moment as though she would burst into tears, aware that she'd been made a fool of at George's expense.

I remember that that night, after dinner, Doris drank a bottle of bordeaux. I watched the wine go gurgling into her glass, a big, stout-stemmed, widemouthed wineglass. She shuffled over to the back door, I remember, and threw it open, and I sat there watching her as she gazed out into the twilit yard, and the birds twittered their evening chorus from the trees over by the barn. She leaned her back against the doorframe, so that I had her profile, in silhouette: she was tall, tall and thin, with a long pointed nose and a receding chin, and her hair was scraped to a tight bun at the nape of her neck. Still outlined sharply against the last light, she raised the glass to her lips and drank. The long, bobbing throat, the slightly concave spine, feet flat on the step and one long hand hanging limp at her side—her body seemed to surrender utterly to the tilted wineglass. She emptied it, then stood a few minutes more, head still thrown back against the doorframe, as the sounds and smells of dusk came drifting in; then she turned her head toward me and heaved a deep sigh. "Ah, Sir Hugo," she murmured, "we've lost him." I sat there grinning at her, and thinking: you're right, you're right.

* * *

Harriet was staying with the Horns, of course, and there were glum faces in that house the night of the fourth day. The next morning the barristers would present their closing arguments, the judge would sum up, and the jury would retire. Victor had followed the case closely in the newspapers, and he was very upset. Or so I imagine. For he liked George Lecky, the pair of them had often talked in the garden of Crook about football, and Africa, and dinosaurs, and the war, and I knew that George, for his part, always took a strong, quiet pleasure, as he went about his work, pipe between his teeth, in the boy's eager questions and lively mind. Even as a very small child Victor had been a friend of George's, and I can remember an afternoon one autumn when, from my bedroom window in the east wing, I'd watched George pushing a wheelbarrow of dead leaves across the back yard, with Victor, aged six, perched fatly atop the load, bouncing up and down and shouting with glee, and clutching George's three-pronged fork like a little god of the sea, an infant Poseidon being borne home across the waves in his chariot. Victor knew that George was incapable of killing anybody; why then did the newspapers say he'd done it?

"Because," said his father, "some newspapers always try to make things worse than they really are. They sell more copies that way."

"Well, if people know that," said Victor, "they won't pay any attention, and Mr. Lecky will be acquitted."

"I wish that were true," said Henry.

And so the last day began. Humphrey Stoker first reviewed the evidence, and demonstrated how deeply it incriminated George. Having made his arguments in a relatively rational tone, he then became histrionic. With some passion he told the jury that a monster capable of such inhuman brutality toward a young man with everything to live for—a young man, he stressed, on the brink of a promising literary career—such a monster deserved the most extreme penalty the law could exact. He for one, he said, would not sleep soundly in his bed until he knew that George Lecky would never walk the land again. He implored the jury neither to flinch nor falter from their duty; and their duty, their terrible duty, he said quietly, he believed, with humility, he had established: they must reach a verdict of guilty, guilty of murder in the first degree. Then he sat down.

Then Sir Fleckley stood up. His learned friend, he said, was perfectly correct. "If you find," he said, "beyond a reasonable doubt that George Lecky murdered Sidney Giblet, then your verdict must indeed be one of guilty. But I wonder, ladies and gentlemen of the jury, whether we cannot say that here, surely, reasonable doubt exists?" He then, at length, and in detail, elaborated upon the circumstantial nature of the evidence, admitting that George had erred, and erred badly, in not reporting the body to the authorities; but that error, he reiterated, was not the same thing as capital murder. And if they had any doubt, any doubt at all, as he was sure they must have, then they must bring in a verdict of not guilty. In his summing up, Mr. Justice Congreve made a similar point; his instructions to the jury in fact revolved around this very point, for none of the evidence had been contested. With watery eyes and quavery voice the little old man then sent them off to deliberate, and the court adjourned.

It took them forty-three minutes to reach their verdict, and a tense forty-three minutes it was. For so eloquent had been Sir Fleckley's closing address, and so emphatically had the judge supported his circumstantiality argument, that fresh hope had sprung up in Harriet's and Hilary's hearts. Mrs. Giblet joined them in the small chamber Sir Fleckley had put at their disposal, adjacent to his own; and for forty-three minutes the three women waited there in an agony of suspense. Sir Fleckley suddenly appeared through the door connecting to his own chambers, the skirts of his robe swirling about his pin-striped trousers. "They're back," he said.

"Guilty of murder in the first degree," said the foreman, and George opened his mouth, drew back his lips, clamped his great teeth together then pressed a hand to his eyes. Yes, he answered Mr. Justice Congreve, he did have something to say before sentence was passed: he was innocent, he had told the truth; and if he died for his crime, he died unjustly. That was all. Harriet and Hilary were not the only ones in the courtroom whose cheeks were damp with tears. Mr. Justice Congreve very slowly donned his white gloves and black cap. His baggy throat, his small, wobbling, wizened head: they seemed such tiny, fragile shreds of flesh to be bearing the weighty majesty of those red robes, that glorious wig with the black cap fitted to the crown. His voice was the voice of an old, old man, unspeakably tired and yearning for death.

"George Kitchener Lecky, you have been found guilty of a terrible crime. The sentence of the court upon you is, that you be taken from this place to a lawful prison, and thence to a place of execution, and that you there be hanged by the neck until you be dead; and that your body be afterwards buried within the precincts of the prison in which you shall have been confined before your execution. And may the Lord have mercy on your soul."

"Amen," said the chaplain of the court, who stood behind the judge and to his left.

THE LONG GRIM shadow of the gallows stretched all the way to Crook, and in the days that followed an eerie stillness settled on the house. Mrs. Giblet was often on the telephone to Harriet, and I understood from conversations in the drawing room that the only hope now was an appeal for clemency that had been put before the Home Secretary. And that was all George had to clutch at as he languished, hollow-eyed and black of heart, in his lonely cell at the core of one of the oldest of England's great prisons. And as I say, we all felt it, at Crook, we all felt the crushing weight of the death sentence. Even Fledge betrayed emotion, on at least one occasion, when dealing with Doris in the kitchen after dinner. It was a mark of the intense strain he was feeling, for as I've indicated, the expression of emotion was anathema to the man. Not passion,

I hasten to add, not the expression of passion. Passion he could express, and did, nightly, and this I imagine helped to divert Harriet from brooding constantly on George's fate. In fact, the routine established in the weeks after my accident was soon in place once more. Doris weaved off to bed well before midnight, having sometimes got me down before passing out herself. After this Fledge would take a turn round the grounds, then lock up, and noiselessly ascend the back stairs with a candle.

Harriet and Fledge were by this time at a point in their relationship where, despite the tensions endemic to their situation, they were subject to an almost uncontrollable physical longing for one another. The touch of a hand, a stray glance, a certain tone of voice—and I would be left alone in the drawing room as the pair slipped out, headed, I have no doubt, either for Fledge's pantry or Harriet's bedroom. I believe he even took her in the dining room once, right after dinner, on the floor, heedless that Doris might enter. Harriet, you see, having finally abandoned all moral and religious scruples, had quickly come to adore the sight of Fledge's fine penis rising stiff and faintly throbbing from that soft fleece of red-brown pubic hair. Herself damp, her upper thighs already smeared with fluid secretions indicative of deep arousal, she would lift her plump-fingered hands to loosen the great coils of copper-colored hair that lay heavily piled atop her skull. She would gaze at the man with immense, inhuman hunger, and then, at last— sweet consummation!—she reached out for him, drew him into her arms, and covered his pale body with her kisses.

Afterwards there would be a spell of languid torpor, and then—oh, how well I knew my Harriet!—her brow would darken as her thoughts fled from the butler in her bed to the gardener in his distant cell. So it was that in the very bower of love arose the specter of death.

George's date of execution was set for May 24, roughly three weeks from sentencing. Having been probed, analyzed, and defined by the police, by the lawyers, by the jury of his peers, and even by the psychiatric community, George was now exclusively the property of the worst sort of newspapers and their public. They called him a brute, a maniac, and a monster. Like a screen he was illuminated by their lurid projections. Cleo read me the stories, and my heart wept for my old African comrade. Nor was it only the press that maintained a relentless scrutiny of the man: in his prison cell George was the object of dozens of pairs of custodial eyes. I, too, saw him, I saw him in my mind's eye, one afternoon in the middle of May. He was sitting on the edge of a low concrete bunk, his elbows on his knees, his long jaw cradled in his palms and his fingertips laid upon his eyelids.

"Lecky."

George is in ill-fitting prison clothes with a number stenciled across the pocket of the shirt. He pulls his fingers down his cheeks, briefly stretching the skin from his eye sockets. Sunlight streams through the barred window and falls in slats across the cell floor, and stripes the hunched form of the man on the bunk. A pair of flies goes endlessly round and round just beneath the ceiling. Slowly straightening his back and laying his palms flat on his knees, George turns to the door and, lit from behind, his face is dark with shadow. From out of this darkness comes a hollow sound, barely recognizable as the once-gruff voice of George Lecky.

"What is it?"

The key turns in the lock and the door swings open. "Someone to see you."

"Who?"

"King George the Sixth, who do you think? On your feet."

George wearily rises. His hair is cropped even shorter than I remember it, and in his long, dour face, particularly around his eyes and in the cleft of his thick eyebrows, can be read a slackening of the man's tight-knit nature, the unmistakable signs of exhaustion and despair. He seems devitalized, enfeebled, unnerved. He shuffles to the door, hitching the loose, baggy prison trousers about his narrow hips, and, stooping slightly, emerges into the corridor.

The warder locks the door behind them and slips his vast bunch of keys, which are linked by a chain to his belt, into a deep side pocket of his trousers. "Come on, Lecky," he says, and the pair of them move down the corridor toward the office at the end of the block, their advancing shadows falling across the hard-edged grids of sunlight that come slicing through cell doors and skylights as the two men go trudging by.

At the end of the cell block stood a senior warder. "You've got a visitor, George," he said. He was an older man, kindly and paternalistic. "Got tobacco, have you, George?"

George nodded.

"Right. Down you go then." He unlocked a grille gate giving onto a steep cast-iron spiral staircase. As George and his warder descended, the gate banged shut behind them and the harsh metallic clangor of the key turning in the lock echoed loudly down the stairwell. At the bottom George stood by while the procedure was repeated; then down a short hallway and into a small square room with a single barred window set high in one wall. The walls were painted a dingy green to chest height, thereafter a sort of off-beige color. In the center of the room stood a sturdy wooden table scarred by cigarette burns; there was a dirty tin ashtray on it, and above it hung a light bulb in a green tin shade. The room was bright with strips and squares of sunshine, and on each side of the table stood a wooden chair. As George entered an old woman on one of those chairs turned toward him and, wrapping her hands about the handle of her walking stick, scrutinized him closely. It was Mrs. Giblet.

I OFTEN FIND myself, in this, Crook's *late* period, as I think of it, wondering what exactly Fledge makes of me. The man himself gives me almost nothing, of course, nor has he since the day he turned my wheelchair to the wall. No, phlegmatic as ever, he demonstrates no sign that, for example, his successful seduction and domination of Harriet afford him pride or pleasure. I wonder if, in addition to his innate sly caution, he is a superstitious man: Does he think, perhaps, that an outward manifestation of feeling might be unlucky, does he think that there are gods or fates supervising the affairs of mortals, and that these supernatural entities delight in the ruin of our projects? (I've certainly begun to harbor such suspicions with regard to my own life.) Does he, therefore, in order to avoid their interference, practice the tight lip, the blank gaze—that repertoire of stiff and formal gestures from which he seems never to deviate? Is this why he acts as he does— is he attempting to pursue his ambitions unnoticed and unchallenged by the gods? I think quite probably it is.

What, then, does he make of me? I clearly pose no further threat to him, for Crook is, I should say, essentially *his* at this stage. I think actually I may function in Fledge's mind as a sort of trophy, rather like the stag's head opposite the clock in the hallway. I think perhaps he sees me as something he has conquered, and thus as a symbol of his potency (and I might as well be stuffed and mounted, given my current condition). But there is something else going on between Fledge and myself, though the only basis I have for saying any of this is the intuition of a chronic and passive observer. For Fledge, remember, is dressing in a manner very similar to my own now; when he glances over from the fireplace, and sees me grinning at him in a tweed jacket almost precisely the same shade and pattern as his, in cavalry twill trousers of an identical beige, with an equally sharp crease, and leather-soled brogues with or-namental perforations on the toe cap, again no different from his own—what does he see? As for my tie, he may well be wearing its brother; I've noticed that the man has been making free with my ties for some time now, and I've cursed Harriet in my heart that she could be-tray me so intimately.

Yes, there he stands, tall and straight and sleek and elegant and handsome and, looking over, he sees— himself. But it is himself transformed, it is a stunted and grinning reflection he sees—as though he has looked into a distorting mirror and found himself turned into a grotesque. I am his grotesque double; he reads in me an outward sign of his own corruption, I am the externalization, the manifestation, the fleshly representation of his true inner nature—which is a deformed and withered thing. He recognizes this—and it fascinates him, to see *his own soul* grinning at him from a corner of the room. At first his shock of self-recognition was intense—*that* was the day he turned my wheelchair to the wall, *that's* why he did it, I now realize—but in time he has come to take a sort of blackly narcissistic pleasure in the image of his own grotesqueness. And this is why I think of myself as his shriveled conscience, I am the atrophied memory of good that is even now fading and shrinking and wasting away before his eyes. For as I sink, so he rises; aware of this, he sees me as a sort of inversion of himself, the negative to his positive. The irony is that in truth *he* is the negative of *me*, for in *me* the good persists, and for all my flaws—and I do not claim to be perfect, never have, I've been a bad husband and an indifferent father—but for all my flaws I have never abandoned moral value. In contrast to the naked cynicism, the violence and the perversity of Fledge, I, a grotesque, can still glimpse the good. Fledge, diabolical man that he is, *enjoys* the spectacle of my decay in his drawing room; and just as the gargoyle on a Gothic church was a defeated demon forced to serve as a sewer, so, inversely, am I forced to serve as a gargoyle in this anti-cathedral, this hell-hall that Fledge has made of Crook. Fledge is the grotesque—not I!

And having thought this, I begin to snort uproariously, and Harriet runs over to thump my bent and brittle spine. One of these days someone's going to thump it so hard the bloody thing will snap in two, and that'll be the end of Sir Hugo, thank God.

They dance now, you know, Harriet and the grotesque, generally as a prelude to sex. He puts a record on the gramophone, then takes Harriet in his arms and the pair of them quite shamelessly foxtrot around the drawing room. The French windows are open, and the sweet rank smells of my wildly overgrown flower garden come drifting in, along with birdsong, much birdsong. The lights have not been turned on yet, and in the gloom of evening the air is rich with the stink of musky blossoms, and sometimes he even foxtrots her out onto the terrace, for I hear their shoes on the flagstones. Fledge dances well, of course, and carries Harriet along with sinuous and effortless grace; it's a prelude to sex, as I say, for after ten minutes or so they invariably slip off to his pantry, and there, I imagine, Fledge settles himself on the chair by the workbench, his trousers and underpants at his ankles and his cock up like a shinbone. Harriet, in her haste and lust, will have abandoned her own underpants even while descending the staircase and then, having hitched her skirt about her waist, she straddles him. They jog up and down, gently at first, but with gathering velocity. Harriet clings to the man, her fingers clutching at his shoulders, his neck, his hair, and then, with her little chin lifted, her eyes closed, her hair coming loose and tumbling about her shoulders, she emits small cries and squawks as she bumps unsteadily toward the first climax of the evening. She finishes with tears streaming down her cheeks, and rains wet kisses on the face of this marvelous man she has found.

Meanwhile I am sitting in the drawing room listening in great agony as the foxtrot record goes round and round and round, no sooner finished that it starts all over again.

BACK IN LONDON, back in prison, George listened in stoic silence to the news that the Home Secretary had refused to reprieve him. He was standing at the end of his bunk, with the window at his back. The Governor stood in the doorway of the cell and imparted the news in somber tones. "I'm sorry, George," he said. He liked George. They all did.

The change in George was by this stage a dramatic one. He'd lost a good deal of weight, and he had been a lean man when he went in. The long blue jaw, the sunken cheeks and the shaven skull—they all rendered his face extremely haggard. The countryman's stride had been transformed by months of confinement into a stooped, uncertain shuffle, and the constant exercise of willpower had made him uncharacteristically tense. He exercised willpower so as not to lose control; the loss of his life seemed preferable, to George, to loss of control. The Governor and the warders recognized this, that he refused to submit to terror, and they respected it. He smoked his pipe almost constantly.

How well I knew that good, solid man—it was the deprivation of fresh air, and soil, and trees, more than anything else that was breaking him down. He'd spent his life outdoors; he'd been a farmer, and before that a soldier, a good soldier, too, and now for months he'd had nothing but a small patch of sky to remind him that the world was made of more than bricks and steel. They took him out to the yard each day for forty minutes, by himself, but it was almost worse than nothing. He tramped around the dusty stones with the pipe clenched firmly between those big strong teeth of his, unaware, fortunately, of the eyes that gazed from every window overlooking the yard. Add to those eyes my eye—my mind's eye—for I too was keeping George under surveillance, in my imagination, though unlike the others I had for him only love, and pity, and compassion. There was a deep bitterness eating away at George's innards, and this depression, this progressive darkening of the spirit, was spiked ever more frequently by waves of sheer giddy panic at the prospect of dying. It was at those moments that he bit fiercely on the stem of his pipe, and clenched his fists until the knuckles blanched. His mind behaved irrationally: he loved the table and chair in his cell, he loved the bed and the chamber pot, the window and the small blue square of sky. He clutched at them all like a drowning man. But then, at the next moment, his thoughts darted ahead and tried to pierce the darkness and know what would happen—

afterwards. George had no religion to speak of, and shunned the prison chaplain, who appeared each day and left a tract or two. It wasn't the loss of the soul that terrified George but the loss of the senses, the loss of the sensible world: hence his sudden fierce spurts of love for the simple chair he sat upon, for the smell of black tobacco, and for the solid warmth in the voice of a warder called Bert. Then the wave would pass, and he would be left with the dull sardonic ache that throbbed behind all his thoughts, and was only kept manageable by the smoking of his pipe. He played endless games of dominoes with Bert, and the hours seemed at times to drag by with painful slowness, at other times to slip away with terrifying speed. He thought about his trial, quite listlessly; he often thought about me, and asked for news of me. Did he understand why I had forsaken him? I hope to God he did. The prison doctor came to examine him, and pronounced him in sound health. Suddenly George realized that he'd had his allotment, that all that remained was to break down his body and create a death. He was forty-nine years old, and on the far side of the prison they had dug his grave.

During this period, after the trial, Mrs. Giblet was working on George—against me. This was why she came to the prison; why else would she visit the man who had fed her hams fattened on the flesh of her own son? She was plotting against me, trying to get George to betray me, suggesting to him, either in subtle and oblique terms, or quite candidly, that he could save himself by indicting me. She was having no success, at this stage, for George was intensely loyal to me, had been since our African days. But there was another factor in all this, and that was the intense *loneliness* that a man in George's position feels. To contemplate one's own imminent death—I speak now from personal experience—while the rest of humanity looks breezily forward to years, decades—indefinite spans: this sets a man apart. There is a sort of solitude that touches every traveler leaving home, a melancholy that lives deep within the sense of excitement or purpose that prompts the journey. Take that melancholy—Is it the primal fear of the hunter leaving the cave? The fear of never returning? Or of returning to a deserted home, or a home in ruins?—take that melancholy and magnify it a thousandfold, and *that* is the sadness and the isolation of the condemned man. I know. And I suspect that Mrs. Giblet was quite canny enough to know it too, and thus to realize just how vulnerable George was.

For George was pathetically grateful that she visited him, I see that now. In the eyes of the world he was a monster, and the visits of this old woman, the *mother* of his supposed victim, were the only sort of external support he had with which to buttress his increasingly fragile sense of *who he was*. Mrs. Giblet functioned in relation to George as Cleo did to me—they shored us up with their faith and enabled us to go on. They gave us back a reflection of ourselves that was not grotesque or monstrous. They allowed us to believe we were still human, still men. With Mrs. Giblet, however, that support had a price.

Time passed, and the strain grew more intense. George's thoughts revolved constantly around this one stark theme: I'm going to swing for what I didn't do.

He began to have doubts. Until this point he had talked to Mrs. Giblet only because she seemed to want to talk—the profound sense of gratification he derived from her visits had less to do with conversation than with the simple fact that she'd come to see him. He hardly even needed to see her—just to know that she'd come was enough. But if it was talk she wanted, then talk he would give her, that clipped, brusque countryman's talk, the only kind George knew. So he talked about Crook, about the weather last winter, the state of the garden, the state of the soil. And when the old woman asked him about *me*—or rather, when she told him what she suspected of me—well, George just sucked on the stem of his pipe and gazed at the ceiling.

And still the days slipped by, and May 24 loomed larger and larger, like some great animal advancing upon him, and him powerless to move out of its path. Up and down the cell he paced, pulling furiously on that much-chewed pipe stem. Bert could no longer tempt him to dominoes, so he sat in placid silence as George paced up and down, up and down that narrow cell. The prison grays flapped about his bony frame like winding sheets.

George at last reached a decision. He sat down across the table from Bert and stared him straight in the eye. "Bert," he said, "you know who done young Giblet?"

A cloud of unease crossed the other man's face. He said nothing.

"I'll tell you, Bert," said George. There was a husky rasp to his voice. This was going against the grain, but he had to do it, now. "Sir Hugo done him, Bert. Not me, Sir Hugo."

There, it was out. He, too, had betrayed me. In terror of losing his life, he had betrayed his old comrade. He sat there, waiting for Bert's reaction. Bert gazed at his face, a small frown etched between his sandy eyebrows. From far away came the clang of a metal door and the rattle of a bunch of keys. It was night. At last he spoke. "Don't get worked up, George," he murmured. "Don't get yourself in a state, not now."

George gaped at the man. With a rather sick sensation, a sensation of dizzying vertigo, it came to him that he wasn't going to be listened to. He began to protest, but he knew, with utter certainty, that it would do no good. He'd left it too late, much, much too late.

Poor George. Even after what he'd done, I still had love and compassion in my heart for the man.

ON THE AFTERNOON of May 23 Cleo brought Herbert to the kitchen. Yes, my old toady friend was still alive and well, still living in a glass tank in my study and being sporadically fed. The dear girl sat at the kitchen table and put before him a saucer of diced chicken entrails, while I sat looking on with that ever-present bloody grin on my face. Doris, meanwhile, was not very steady on her pins, having been at the gin a little earlier. Something of a novelty for Doris, gin, and her susceptibility to the stuff was distressingly evident. Back and forth she lurched on the other side of the table, a large sharp chopper in one hand and, on the cutting board in front of her, a plucked chicken.

It was a warm afternoon and we had the back door open, and all was tranquil enough, I suppose, apart from this unsteadiness of Doris's. Cleo didn't seem to notice, engrossed as she was with Herbert, and I think I must have dozed off, for it was with a rude shock, as though I had awoken from a dream, that I suddenly heard Doris shout out with pain. I opened my eyes: there she stood, the chopper in her right hand, gazing with astonishment at her left hand, which she held up in front of her face. She had chopped half the index finger clean off. It lay on the table beside the cutting board. There was a good deal of blood around it, and also on the chicken. Cleo was paying no attention at all, but instead sat gazing, her hands flat on the table and her chin on her hands, at Herbert, who had hopped from his saucer of entrails to Doris's severed finger and was lapping at the puddle of blood around the thing with his long flickering amphibian tongue. Doris sank into a chair and sat there in a daze, and watched the blood oozing thickly from the stump of her finger. I sat there grinning at the woman as, with her good hand, she reached down to the floor and picked up the gin bottle and poured herself a stiff one.

George, meanwhile, was pacing up and down the condemned cell. Up and down he paced, up and down. Bert was disappointed in George. He thought he was made of sterner stuff. The chaplain came, for this was May 23, and George had one day left to live. George told him it was I who'd "done" Sidney Giblet—he couldn't help it, in his terror of death he would say anything. The chaplain tried to turn his thoughts to the state of his immortal soul, but with no success. The doctor came, and he too was subjected to an impassioned harangue. The word went quickly round the prison, as these things will, that George Lecky had cracked. It made men sad. For in a way he died for all of them.

When Mrs. Giblet visited George that afternoon she found him in a mood very different from the brusque taciturnity she had come to expect. There had even been some doubt as to whether he should be allowed to see her; finally the visit was approved, but the warders were instructed to take George back to his cell if he became at all excited. They warned George of this before they took him down.

George was no sooner seated in that dingy little visitors' room than he seized Mrs. Giblet's hands across the table and began to speak. Nobody, I think, myself included, had even heard George speak as he must have spoken that afternoon. When he had finished Mrs. Giblet hurriedly left the room, made several telephone calls from the front office of the prison, then took a taxi to Waterloo Station. She was coming to Crook.

Difficult to say how long I sat in the kitchen watching Doris drink gin while the stump of her finger bled all over the chicken. Twenty minutes, maybe more, maybe an hour. Eventually Fledge came down the hall. He quickly took in the scene, his eyes darting from the blood on the table, to Doris, to Cleo, to myself, then back to the blood; and it was all too easy to understand the quick twitch of contempt that touched his lips. His intoxicated wife looked on dumbly as her own blood dripped steadily onto a plucked chicken, and watching it all, in utter passivity, grinning and withered and huddled like a heap of old sticks in a suit of clothes now vastly too large for his slumped and shrunken frame, sat the master of the house. In his place I too should have twitched with contempt. To be reduced to such flaccid inertia! My eyes, I know, were sunk now deep in shadowy, hollow sockets; my cheekbones protruded sharply from a face that had all the brittle and yellowy consistency of parchment; I was stubbled and food-stained and drooling, and altogether like a grubby little caterpillar as I clung grimly to existence in my housing of tweed. And did nothing; Cleo and I, myself and my elf, we sat there and did nothing. It was as though my own eye, like the halibut's, had migrated, shifted into Fledge's skull to witness the state to which we'd been reduced.

Things happened quickly after that. Briskly and competently Fledge disinfected and bandaged Doris's wound, then telephoned the doctor. As I heard him replace the receiver there was a loud rap at the front door. I heard him go down the hall. I saw the front door open, and standing on the threshold was Mrs. Giblet. There was an obscure buzz of voices, and they entered the drawing room. Less than a minute later Fledge reappeared in the kitchen, took my chair by the handles and wheeled me down the hall. I was placed against the drawing room wall, facing the fireplace. Mrs. Giblet and Harriet were standing in the middle of the room, Harriet perturbed and the old woman in a state of some impatience. Fledge withdrew, closing the door behind him.

"Time is very short, Lady Coal," said Mrs. Giblet. "I am afraid we must dispense with the niceties—a man's life hangs in the balance."

240

"But what is all this?" said Harriet. "Won't you at least sit down, Mrs. Giblet? A cup of tea?"

"I have come straight from Wandsworth, Lady Coal. George Lecky told me what happened the night Sidney disappeared."

I felt some pain in my chest, a rather vivid burning pain that spread across the top of my body like a set of tentacles, tentacles of flame. "But surely we know—?" murmured Harriet.

"George Lecky did not tell the truth," said Mrs. Giblet. "He was trying to protect your husband, Lady Coal."

"But protect him from *what*, precisely, Mrs. Giblet?" Harriet gazed at me, then sank into an armchair, her hands folded in her lap and a small frown picked between her eyebrows as she turned to Mrs. Giblet.

"From the consequences of his actions, Lady Coal. Sir Hugo came to George Lecky's farmhouse that night; he was in a very bad state."

"Very bad?" said Harriet faintly.

"Shocked, excited. And he had been drinking. He said there had been an accident, and that George must come back to Crook with him. George agreed; he followed Sir Hugo back in his swill lorry. They parked halfway up the drive. Sir Hugo led him into the trees. In a shallow depression, partially covered with leaves, lay the body of my son, Lady Coal. His throat had been cut."

"Oh good God!" cried Harriet. Her hands flew to her lips and she turned toward me with wide, horrified eyes.

"They carried Sidney to the lorry and crammed him

into a dustbin, Lady Coal. They threw the bicycle up after him. George said Sidney's neck had been cut so deeply he feared the head would come away from the body.'' The voice was firm as a rock—not a quaver, not a tremor. "Then he drove back to Ceck's Bottom, and they did together what George said in court that he had done alone.''

The pain in my chest had suddenly subsided, and been replaced by a sort of tingling numbness, all over the top half of my body. Poor George; once he'd cracked he would have said anything to escape the gallows. This thin piece of horror by moonlight—the pity of it was that Harriet appeared to be swallowing it whole. She continued to stare at me as though she were seeing me for the first time. But so weary was I by now, so ready to let it all slip from my hands, I could barely summon a twinge of outrage that she should view me in this light, and I with no chance to tell her the truth.

"But why?'' Harriet was saying. "Why would Hugo want to murder Sidney?''

The pain in my chest had disappeared; now, only that numbness. "According to George Lecky," said Mrs. Giblet slowly, and looking intently at me, "Sir Hugo was being blackmailed by my son, Lady Coal.''

A brief silence descended as the three of us contemplated this bizarre piece of nonsense. Oh how desperate that poor man was, to twist the truth like this! Had Fledge gotten to him, too? I no longer cared. The pain in my chest had passed, but I could feel the first convulsions of a snorting fit begin to rock my frame. Within a few seconds I was in a state of helpless paroxysm, and Harriet, wifely solicitude overcoming whatever involuntary sensation of horror the old woman's words had aroused in her, was beside me and slapping my back. Mrs. Giblet continued to stare intently at me.

When the fit was over Harriet appeared to have recovered her common sense. She sat in her armchair and said: "But this is incredible. Why would Sidney blackmail Hugo? Whatever for? And why do you say these things, Mrs. Giblet? What good can they do now, these—wild accusations?"

Mrs. Giblet reluctantly turned from me and sank into the armchair opposite Harriet's. Wrapping her claws about the crook of her stick, she heaved a sigh of great weariness. There followed a long silence, and I had the distinct impression that the old woman was debating with herself whether to voice more of her grotesque suspicions. "Perhaps none," she murmured at last. "Perhaps none at all. A man's life hangs in the balance, Lady Coal," she said again. "It had occurred to me that if Sir Hugo were confronted with what George Lecky had sworn to me is the truth, it might somehow unblock him."

"Unblock him?" said Harriet slowly. "Unblock him? But this is not possible, Mrs. Giblet, this I have been told on best authority, and God knows—"

"Quite, Lady Coal, quite," said the old woman. "But I simply could not rule out the possibility that Sir Hugo's paralysis was hysterical."

"Hysterical!"

Mrs. Giblet turned to me again for a moment, and then began to fumble in her coat for cigarettes. "Apparently not," she said quietly.

It was then that the doctor arrived.

I SPENT THE night in considerable distress, not least because I suffered fresh outbreaks of those burning pains in my chest. To suggest that I was being blackmailed by Sidney—absurd! I, the invert? I, the murderer? Quite absurd. You know my feelings about Fledge—I merely embody his monstrousness, make salient his inner deformity, and thus mirror his nature.

George was hanged shortly after eight o'clock the following morning. He found peace, I hope; God knows, he'd had little enough since the day he cracked in prison. The atmosphere in Crook was bleak; Cleo had withdrawn to her room, and Doris, her finger heavily bandaged and her arm in a sling, sat in the kitchen and stared out at the day, which was windy and fresh. The doctor had not attempted to sew the finger back together, it had apparently been off too long. We had scrambled eggs for lunch, cooked by Harriet. After lunch I was wheeled down the hall and into the drawing room and over to the French windows. The pain in my chest had suddenly disappeared, as it had the day before, to be replaced by a spreading numbness. It was then that I saw George in the garden.

I have spoken to you of these sightings. They are phantoms, projections, this I know, but nevertheless they feel real. George was not alone this time; he was standing at the head of a great crowd, a crowd that completely filled the garden and pushed up against the walls on every side. They jostled and shuffled slightly, and they all, without exception, were gazing up at me, where I sat on the terrace outside the French windows. The air was thick with birds, for some reason, thrushes and sparrows, and even some crows. A light breeze touched the trees beyond the garden wall, and a few thin white clouds went drifting and kicking across the sky. Who were these people? George was in his work clothes, his old frayed pin-striped jacket and his brown corduroy trousers. The men and women who clustered so closely about him, they too were in work clothes. They were country folk, farm folk, and I could make no sense of their shuffling, silent presence in my flower garden.

I remember reading somewhere that the living are just a rare species of the dead. I don't believe this. The living, I think, are *larvae* of the dead—dead bodies at an early stage of development. But why should I have thought of this now—were these the dead thronging my garden? Harriet and Fledge had brought their coffee down to the drawing room and were sitting by the fireplace, talking in low tones about George, I think. After a few minutes I heard Fledge cross the room to the drinks cabinet. Getting out the brandy, I presume, and he certainly had cause to celebrate, the case of Sidney Giblet having now been closed. He had got away with murder, and was now the undisputed master of Crook. In his place, I too should have had a brandy.

I shall be buried in the Ceck churchyard, beside my mother, and my funeral, I imagine, will be only slightly better attended than my lecture. Paleontologists hate to bury things, especially bones; I'm sure I don't have to tell you why. Poor George will not have done so well: an unmarked lime pit within the prison walls, this is where he'll have been laid to rest. I do worry about Cleo; I've told you we Coals have a tendency to despair, and I'm rather afraid that with me out of the picture it may well get the better of her. I'm rather afraid she'll go the way of Sir Digby.

Fledge has turned on the gramophone, and is asking Harriet if she will dance. That numbness in my upper body: it feels now as though I have been suffused with a great light. In the garden, George has begun to rise from the ground. Very slowly he ascends, to a height of about ten or twelve feet, and as he does so he very slowly opens his arms. They are all still gazing at me, but from George's eyes, and ears, and mouth, and from the region of his heart, a sort of silvery radiance is spilling forth, dazzling me and filling me with a sensation of immense, oceanic peace, a quite extraordinary feeling of bliss. He is surrounded by fluttering birds, barely visible in this blinding, gorgeous light. What is happening to me? *Nil desperandum*, I hear myself murmur, as behind me Harriet and Fledge begin dancing the foxtrot, and continue to do so throughout this unsettled afternoon, as the wind freshens, and wails about the gables of Crook, blowing from the south.

About the Author

PATRICK McGRATH was born in London and grew up near Broadmoor Hospital, where for many years his father was Medical Superintendent. He has lived in various parts of North America, and for several years on a remote island in the north Pacific. He moved to New York City in 1981. He is the author of the critically acclaimed collection *Blood and Water and Other Tales*. *The Grotesque* is his first novel.